LARA CROFT
TOMB
RAIDER
THE CRADLE OF LIFE

A novelisation by Nancy Krulik

Based on a Story by

Kirk M. Petruccelli & Lloyd Levin and James V. Hart

Screenplay by Dean Georgaris

London   New York   Sydney

First published in Great Britain in 2003 by Pocket Books
An imprint of Simon & Schuster UK Ltd
Africa House, 64-78 Kingsway, London WC2B 6AH

Originally published in the USA in 2003 by Aladdin Paperbacks,
An imprint of Simon & Schuster Children's Publishing Division, New York.

POCKET BOOKS and colophon are registered trademarks of Simon & Schuster
A CIP catalogue record for this book is available from the British Library.

ISBN 07434 7807 X

13579108642

Printed and bound in Great Britain by Cox & Wyman Ltd, Reading, Berkshire

PROLOGUE

Crash!

An empty wineglass fell from the table, but none of the guests even seemed to notice. These things happened all the time at Greek weddings—the music was playing and the people were dancing. It was only natural that the vibrations should cause some of the china to fall from the tables.

As the guests danced around in the wedding tent, the glasses on the table began to shake more wildly. One by one they crashed to the ground, breaking into small shards of fine crystal. The wedding cake fell to the floor in a mass of crushed icing and whipped cream. Then the canopy above began to sway back and forth. Any minute now it seemed that the entire taverna would plunge into the sea.

This, however, wasn't the result of heavy-footed dancing. This was an earthquake. An earth-shattering event that not only upset a wedding, but would alter events worldwide.

Naturally, Lara Croft couldn't be far behind. . . .

CHAPTER ONE

Nicholas Petraki and his brother Jimmy stood on the deck of their salvage boat, *Konstantinos,* and watched as a crew of Greek sailors hauled an ancient statue from the sea.

"They found another one!" Nicholas called down to his father, Gus.

"Mark their location!" Gus shouted from the pilot seat of the boat.

Nicholas did as he was told. He'd been marking locations all morning. Ever since the earthquake yesterday, strange artifacts had been springing to the surface of the sea. Certainly ancient objects weren't unheard of in Greece. But these objects had never been seen before. They'd obviously been shaken loose from some ancient underwater kingdom by the force of the quake. Archaeologists from all over the world would be arriving soon to marvel at them. And they wouldn't be the only ones coming to Greece.

Tomb raiders would surely be arriving as well. In fact, some had already arrived. It was the usual cast of characters, Gus thought. The Frenchmen and the Kristos family. Gus sighed as he dialed a number on his cell phone. "They're all here," he moaned as he listened to the busy signal coming from his phone. "All except one!" Gus looked at his watch. It was getting late. There would be nothing left if they didn't get a move on. "Follow Kristos," he told his sons finally. "When he dives, we dive. Maybe we'll get lucky and find whatever . . ."

But before Gus could finish his sentence, his words were drowned out by the sound of a Jet Ski zooming up behind them. Instantly the three Petraki men turned to see who had arrived.

A big smile came over their faces as the jet skier came closer. Her long dark hair and shining eyes were unmistakable.

"Better late than never," Nicholas said to his brother.

"Why isn't she slowing down?" Jimmy asked nervously, as the woman drew closer and closer to the *Konstantinos*. The small boat began to toss back and forth as the Jet Ski caused bigger and bigger waves. *Whoosh!* The skier broke sharply and showered the Petraki brothers with water.

"You were asking?" Nicholas grimaced, as he wiped the saltwater from his eyes.

Suddenly the skier spun back and, using a wave as a ramp, leaped up into the air. She flew toward the boat, and, after a front flip, landed neatly beside the boat.

As Lara Croft climbed gracefully up the ladder of his boat, Gus Petraki frowned. "Half the world's raiders are already here," he reprimanded her. "You make us wait."

"You know I can't resist a bit of fun," she told him in her crisp British accent. Then, seeing that he still looked quite upset, she softened her tone and flashed him a bright smile. "Forgive me?"

Gus waited a moment and then broke into a laugh, patting her cheek. He couldn't stay angry with Lady Croft for very long. Lara was truly one of his favorite people. She was one of the world's leading archaeological experts, despite her relatively young age. That's because she was a true adventuress. There was very little Lara couldn't figure out, and even less that frightened her.

In fact, Lady Lara Croft seemed to thrive on danger . . . a trait she got from her late father along with his love of antiquities. So it was no coincidence that she was now about to embark on yet another search for long-lost treasures of a forgotten world.

Seeing Gus smiling so proudly at her, the young tomb raider grinned and then turned her attention to the soaking wet Petraki brothers. They were busy bringing her diving gear up onto the deck of the *Konstantinos*. "You two ought to know me better," she teased, laughing as she watched them shaking water from their hair.

As soon as Lara's gear was onboard, she and the Petrakis began to plan out their diving strategy. "Lara, tell us," Gus said as they gathered around a small table near the portside of the boat. "What's all this fuss about? What do they think is down there?"

Lara reached into her backpack and pulled out a stack of reproductions of ancient drawings. "The Luna Temple," Lara replied, dropping the drawings on the table.

Gus's eyes grew wide. "The Luna Temple," he whispered with a combination of awe and amazement.

Obviously Gus was well aware of the stories behind the Luna Temple. And just as obviously, his sons were clueless. Gus rolled his eyes. "My sons," he complained to Lara. "If it's not on TV, forget it!"

"It's a temple built by Alexander the Great," Lara explained to Nicholas and Jimmy.

"Who was Greek in case you didn't know," Gus barked at them.

"Alexander collected treasures from all over the world. He stored them in two places." Lara pointed to one of the drawings, a map of Alexander the Great's empire. "The majority went to his library in Egypt, which the Romans torched in an act of historical stupidity. But his most prized possessions went here. . ." She spread out a series of drawings of a temple filled with artifacts. In the center was a giant statue of Alexander himself. "The Luna Temple. By law no one was allowed to record its location. Then in 300 B.C. it was—"

"Swallowed by the sea," Gus interrupted, an ominous tone in his voice.

Lara nodded. "Destroyed by a volcanic eruption," she added, giving a more scientific explanation for the Temple's disappearance. "Lost forever. Until yesterday. If even half of that temple is intact, this will be the greatest find since the pyramids."

Jimmy and Nicholas exchanged glances. Dollar signs practically fell from their eyes. Immediately the brothers grabbed a nautical chart and began plotting a course.

"The others are heading here, along this shelf," Jimmy said, following a route with his finger.

"That's based on the currents?" Lara asked him.

The brothers nodded. Lara pulled out a satellite photo and spread it across the table.

"This is why I was late," she explained. "It's a geographical photo taken two hours after the quake. The epicenter was here, five miles northeast of us." She pointed at a small circle on the picture. "Look at the currents along the shelf now."

"They've shifted," Nicholas noted.

Jimmy grinned as he began to understand the significance of what Lara was saying. "So while they're all diving there, the ruins will actually be . . ."

Lara tapped a spot on the map that was quite far from where the other boats were located. If her calculations were correct, the whole Luna Temple would be left for the taking! Instantly Jimmy and Nicholas leaped from the table and ran for their diving gear.

"That is the fastest I have ever seen them move," Gus said, laughing as he prepared to go back to the pilot seat of the boat.

Lara left to change into her diving suit and to prepare her weapons—a spear pistol and an underwater firing gun which had been designed especially for her. They were all the ammunition she'd need. Lara was traveling light on this mission.

As she came down from the wheelhouse, she spotted Gus staring pensively out at the sea. "Something wrong?" she asked, her dark eyes searching his face.

Gus let out a deep sigh. "First Alexander doesn't record its location. Then God wipes it from the Earth with a volcano. Did it ever occur to you that maybe this temple's not meant to be found?"

Lara shook her head. "Everything's meant to be found," she assured him.

CHAPTER TWO

Lara climbed onto her diving sled and descended into the sea. She was followed close behind by Jimmy and Nicholas. The boys were excited, anxious to see what riches awaited them in the Luna Temple. But they were also nervous. This was uncharted territory. Neither of them had been on a dive in this part of the water, and the terrain seemed more dangerous than they were used to, full of underwater cliffs and tunnels, forged by centuries of small earthquakes and other seismic activity.

Lara, as usual, was fearless. As the trio approached an underwater cliff, the brothers slowed to evaluate the danger. Lara, on the other hand, rolled sideways, slipped between them, and dove off the edge of the cliff with no hesitation whatsoever. The brothers could do nothing other than follow her lead.

They rode along among the fish until they came upon a narrow, dark, foreboding tunnel in the rock. Jimmy and Nicholas pulled back and looked at Lara. Without saying a word their message was clear—*after you.*

Lara didn't hesitate. She took the lead, maneuvering through the narrow tunnel. Jimmy followed close behind, and Nicholas took up the rear. The tunnel was so tight, the raiders had to lay flat on their sleds to make it through.

At first, the tunnel seemed like a wrong turn. There was no sign of the Temple anywhere. There was nothing but rock, coral, and cold darkness.

Then suddenly Lara spotted a few fragments of tile along the floor of the tunnel. She looked to the left. There was a chunk of an ancient column embedded in the rock. A sense of excitement took over Lara's body. Her heart started to beat just a little faster, and the blood seemed to move a little quicker through her veins. Lara had felt this way before. They were about to discover something marvelous— she could just feel it.

But before Lara could discover anything, she would have to get through the tunnel. And that wasn't going to be easy considering a mass of coral had fallen from the roof and was blocking her path.

Lara Croft was not about to let some underwater sea

life keep her from being the first person to enter the Luna Temple in thousands of years. With a flick of her wrist, she gunned the throttle of her sled, and smashed straight through the wall of coral!

Lara soon found herself floating on the surface of the water in a deep underground air pocket. She tilted her sled so its front spill light could illuminate the area. As she looked around her, a huge grin formed on her face. She had found her way into an elegant, regal room. Sure, the tiles were broken, and some of the statues had cracked, but there was no mistaking where she was: The tunnel had led them straight up through a hole in the floor of the Temple.

The Temple itself was no longer the sturdy structure Alexander the Great had once created. Years of underwater erosion and tremors had caused it to tilt to one side. There were countless small leaks in the ceiling, as well. But for the most part, the Temple was intact, untouched for thousands of years.

Jimmy and Nicholas began to laugh with excitement. The Temple was filled with gold and silver objects just waiting to be taken up to the surface. No other boat was anywhere nearby. This treasure was all theirs! The brothers dismounted their sleds and headed for a huge pile of jewels.

Jimmy and Nicholas went into action, filling their bags with as much bounty as they could carry—silver sextants, black pearls, and golden bowls.

"I could get used to this tomb raiding," Nicholas mused as he placed another strand of black pearls into his sack. "Lara, what do you say to two handsome Greek partners?"

But Lara was too focused on something else to answer. She approached a large seated statue of Alexander the Great. "I'll be gentle," she said to him. She then focused on some drawings that were used to decorate the wall. In all her experience with tomb raiding, Lara had never seen anything like these. She turned on her Digi-cam and began to record the strange symbols and drawings. They seemed to be telling a story about Alexander's journey, but it was hard to say for sure.

One drawing in particular caught her eye. It was of an army of fallen soldiers, but it didn't appear that any of the soldiers had been wounded in war. They just seemed to have died right where they stood, for no obvious reason. Among the bodies was a small box, like a treasure chest. "Bad day," Lara half joked as she filmed the image.

Lara moved over and began to explore the statue of Alexander. It had obviously been crafted by a fine artist of his time. But there was something strange about one of the statue's eyes. As she got closer to it, Lara noticed that the pupil of one of the eyes was covered by a medallion. She reached up and took it in her hand. Lara's sharp eyes studied the carving on the medallion. It showed a figure playing some sort of musical instrument.

As Lara studied the medallion, the flashlight on her belt slipped, and the beam pointed up into the darkness. Lara gasped as the room became filled with a kaleidoscope of reflected light.

Quickly, Lara scanned the Temple, searching for the source of the rotating rainbow of colors. It was then that she noticed the shining Orb sitting on a black conic base and encased by a cage of iron high atop the Temple. Quietly, she pointed her flashlight up toward the Orb.

"How did you see that?" Nicholas asked her, assuming she had purposely aimed her light at the Orb.

"I'm a professional," Lara replied, completely deadpan, as she put down her guns, removed most of her gear, and set the medallion down beside her pack.

"Alex, how about a boost," she joked as she leaped up onto the statue of Alexander the Great and began her ascent toward the Orb. Using the statue's hand as a platform, Lara was able to scale the sloping wall of the Temple. She climbed slowly, careful not to jostle any of the beams that held the room together. Instinctively Lara knew that one false move could prove disastrous for them all.

As she reached the point on the wall that was closest to the Orb, Lara deftly stretched her long, lean body and grabbed for the cage. Bracing herself she turned and looked down. She gasped as she saw that there was a giant figure drawn on the floor. It was a nebulous being, shadowlike, and horrifying. Lara had never seen anything like it before.

Quickly Lara switched her focus back to the Orb. She was suddenly anxious to finish her work here. The tomb raider removed a small acetylene torch from her belt and pre-pared to cut the metal cage that imprisoned the Orb. Before she could even begin to cut, the Temple began to shake.

"Aftershock!" Jimmy cried out. He ducked, trying to avoid bits of falling ceiling.

Lara grabbed onto the cage and held on tightly to keep from falling. She tried not to focus on the column off to the side that was currently separating from its base. At any moment, the whole Temple could collapse on them.

"I think that's a sign to leave," Jimmy said, as the after-shock subsided to a stop.

Nicholas looked at the water streaming into the Temple. A pool had already formed at the lower side of room. "I think that's a sign to leave fast!"

Lara had to agree with the brothers. But something in her would not allow her to leave the Temple without that Orb. "Two minutes," she told the brothers.

Nicholas and Jimmy stared at Lara in amazement. Was she insane? Still, they wouldn't leave without her. The brothers nodded and went back to gathering jewels—faster now.

Lara fired up her torch and began carving away at the metal cage. The noise was deafening, and the sparks were flying in every direction. Lara was so focused on her work that she never noticed the team of six men entering the Temple through a break in the floor.

Within seconds the intruders held the unsuspecting Petraki brothers prisoner. The brothers struggled valiantly, but they were no match for the spears, pistols, and knives their captors waved so expertly.

One of the group's leaders, a man known as Chen Lo, aimed his spear pistol toward Lara.

"Lara! Watch out!" Jimmy screamed at the top of his lungs. Those were his last words.

Lara looked down, stunned. She could do nothing but watch with horror as Xien, Chen Lo's brother, stabbed Nicholas.

Lara had little time to mourn her friends. She shoved off from the Orb cage, sending it swinging, and grabbed onto the wall just as the first wave of spears flew by her. The spears seemed to encircle her, landing only inches from her head and body. One came so close, it ripped her diving suit.

Obviously Chen Lo's henchmen were experts in the art of murder.

Chen Lo eyed Lara, then reached down and picked up her gear and the medallion she had taken from the Temple. Trapped up high on the wall, there was little she could do to stop him. Her only chance at survival was to dive into the pool of water that was now rising within the walls of the Luna Temple.

Lara grabbed the Orb from the cage and used one of the cage's bars to swing down into the water. She lost her grip and dropped the Orb behind the statue, out of reach. Her form was almost perfect as she started downward. She landed with a splash.

Within seconds Chen Lo and his men blindly fired spears into the water, hoping to hit Lara. Lara was quick, though, and she managed to avoid the spears at every turn.

As she darted from side to side, Lara noticed something Chen Lo had missed. While he'd been busy stealing most of Lara's gear and the medallion, he'd not seen her underwater firing gun, which was submerged in the rising water. Talk about luck! Lara swam for the lone weapon at top speed.

Grabbing the gun Lara released the safety and turned around. *Bang!* Without ever leaving the water Lara was able to shoot one of the attackers.

While Chen Lo's men were hunting for Lara, he

searched for the Orb. He had seen it fall as Lara hit the water. It didn't take him long to find the treasure and return his attention to Lara. Quickly he aimed his spear gun straight for her. Instantly his remaining henchmen did the same.

Lara aimed her gun right back at them . . . and then realized that she was outnumbered. Of course that had never stopped Lara in the past.

She spun around and fired her last shot at the weakened Temple column. *Blam!* She shot out its base. The entire Temple began to collapse.

Having gotten what he came for, Chen Lo now had to get out alive with the Orb. Quickly he fired his spear gun at Lara's sled, and the oxygen tank emptied in seconds. His men grabbed the remaining water sleds the Petraki brothers had brought along on the dive and disappeared into a nearby tunnel. They never once looked back, even as they heard the Temple ceiling collapse on top of Lara Croft!

CHAPTER THREE

Lara managed to escape being crushed to death by the ceiling and columns of the Luna Temple. But as she crawled painfully toward a hole in the Temple floor, she realized that Chen Lo had stolen the sleds and disabled her air tank. She was deep underwater. There was no chance she could hold her breath long enough to reach the surface.

Of course, the words "no chance" had never meant anything to Lara. It was simply another challenge—a dare. And Lara could never refuse a dare.

Working feverishly Lara used her knife to cut a small incision in her arm. Then she swam off quickly, leaving a trail of blood behind her. It took only a few seconds to attract a hungry shark.

The shark swam right for Lara. She punched it in the

nose with her left hand and grabbed its fin with her right hand and held on tight. Instinctively the shark bolted toward the surface of the water, dragging Lara along with it.

The tomb raider held on for dear life. The shark was moving quickly now. The world around her began to blur, both from the sheer speed of the animal, and from the dizziness that comes when the brain is refused the oxygen it needs. Just as her breath was about to run out, the shark hit the surface of the water. Lara used her last ounce of strength to explode into the air. She looked around desperately for a sign of the *Konstantinos*. Surely Gus must still be waiting there.

But the boat had disappeared. Lara was stranded in the middle of sea. She could feel herself growing woozy and disoriented, and she began to drift in and out of consciousness. Instinctively she reached for something to hold on to, something to keep her afloat.

From the corner of her eye Lara spotted a large piece of driftwood in the water. She draped her body across it to keep her head out of the water and pulled the cord on her collar that would activate her emergency transmitter.

And then Lara Croft fainted.

Lara had no idea how long she'd been out, but when she opened her eyes again, the bright Greek daylight had given way to a fantastic sunset. It was dusk. She was thirsty, bleeding, and very weak.

Lara sensed danger and looked around—nothing for miles. Then she looked down. A giant shadow was rising to the surface. It was cold, metallic, huge . . . and directly beneath her. There was no way the tomb raider could escape. The monster rose from the sea, carrying Lara on its back.

A submarine! Lara's mind raced. This was no monster. She was already atop the submarine's hull, holding on for dear life as the ship rocked its way to the surface.

Suddenly a hatch opened at the top of the submarine. Two strong arms reached up and yanked Lara inside.

Lara's eyes scanned the face of her captor. Her concern turned to relief as she recognized his caring brown eyes. This was no enemy. This was Hillary, her trusted butler and friend. Obviously he had received her emergency transmission and come to rescue her—along with several members of the British Navy.

Hillary immediately went into action. He poured Lara a cup of hot tea. "Drink if you can," he said, his usually brisk voice softening.

Like a child Lara did as she was told. But before she could get two sips of tea into her, she heard a second familiar voice.

"This is awful!" Lara's friend and equipment designer, Bryce, exclaimed as he studied the broken camera equipment dangling from her shoulders. Bryce was completely unaware of what Lara had just been through. All he could focus on was her trashed camera. "I spend countless hours making sure you have the best equipment. I don't think you appreciate that . . ."

"Bryce," Hillary warned.

"That means you don't appreciate *me*," Bryce continued, refusing to heed Hillary's tone.

Wham! Lara reached out and with a single swipe, knocked Bryce to the ground.

No doubt about it—Lara was down, but she was certainly not out!

CHAPTER FOUR

At the very moment Hillary and Bryce were fishing Lara out of the sea, Dr. Jonathan Reiss was miles away over the Atlantic Ocean, fishing for money. Dr. Reiss rarely had any trouble coming up with funds. He was one of the world's most brilliant scientists, who had chosen to sell his talents to the highest bidder. And the "good guys" were *never* the highest bidder.

This time there were six potential backers from a variety of ethnic backgrounds. They were as cold and calculating as he. Reiss had invited them to fly in his private jet where they were scheduled to have a presentation from the famed scientist. But Dr. Reiss didn't seem to be on the jet. Or at least he hadn't made his presence known.

"Ridiculous!" Mr. Monza, a huge, gluttonous man

bellowed. "Did any of you know he'd moved the meeting to . . . this?" he pointed to the cabin of the Gulfstream G-V jet.

Just then a dark-haired young woman poured Mr. Monza a glass of wine. She avoided eye contact with him as she did her job. He was frightening and he made her nervous.

But Mr. Monza certainly wanted her to pay attention to him. He purposely knocked over the wineglass, forcing her to refill it. As she did, he sneered. "I'm sorry, angel, if I seem irritated. I am not patient like my friends," he snarled at her. "I don't like it when plans are changed for no reason . . ."

"Really, Mr. Monza, I should think you know me better than that."

All heads turned toward the doorway as Jonathan Reiss emerged from behind the curtain. He certainly made quite an entrance. It was impossible not to focus on such a tall, menacing man, with dark, slicked-back hair, and small, penetrating gray eyes.

"Behind every choice I make, one will always find a reason," Dr. Reiss continued in his signature calm, collected tone. Jonathan Reiss was not an excitable man. "In this instance the six of you in one room makes for a tempting target for NATO. Rather than move any of you I decided to move the room at six hundred miles per hour."

Mr. Monza banged angrily on the table with his fist. "That's not an apology!" he bellowed. "It's our money that pays for the shirt on your back, not to mention this jet! Yet you make us wait like dogs!"

The room was quiet now, as tensions were rising. Surely Dr. Reiss would not tolerate such an outburst.

Or would he? Dr. Reiss seemed completely nonplussed by Mr. Monza's accusations. "I apologize, Mr. Monza," Jonathan Reiss said sincerely. Then he turned his attention to the entire group. "Gentlemen, there is an expression that goes, 'It's not nice to fool Mother Nature.' And yet that is precisely what I've been doing. Whether it be sarin gas for Mr. San, improved typhoid for Mr. Krev to use in the Balkans, or enhanced cholera for Mr. Duvalier." He walked around the table slowly, focusing his attention on each man for but a second. "And while those weapons served their purpose, there are always limitations; stable diseases aren't lethal, deadly ones burn out too quickly. Mother Nature can only be fooled so much."

Dr. Reiss paused for a second and glanced at the clock on the wall. Then he took a breath and continued. "After years of fighting her, I've surrendered," he admitted. "Rather than take a disease and attempt to transform it into a weapon of mass destruction, I've gone and found the one weapon nature ever gave us. Something meant for more than scaring the public into wearing gloves when they open their mail. This is the way Mother Nature levels nations." Dr. Reiss stopped for a moment and let his words register with his guests.

But Mr. Monza, for one, was less than impressed with Dr. Reiss's presentation. "Garbage!" He laughed aloud at the ludicrousness of it all. "We've come all this way to hear garbage. Forgive my crude outburst, Doctor, but for years men like you have promised such a weapon and for years they've failed."

"You've never heard the promise from me," Dr. Reiss replied in a measured voice.

Mr. Monza laughed, and then began to cough violently. Dr. Reiss ignored Mr. Monza's discomfort and continued his presentation. "Gentlemen, your governments have attacked their enemies. Those enemies fought back. You've terrorized their citizens, those citizens rallied around waving flags. Deploy my weapon, and those same citizens will tremble at the sight of one another. As they begin to die, they'll blame their own government. Looting will erupt. Murders." Dr. Reiss smiled at the beauty of his plan for his own private Armageddon. "Your enemies, however great, will collapse from within like a house of cards. Or like—"

Dr. Reiss's speech was interrupted by the hacking cough coming from Mr. Monza. Everyone turned and stared as Monza coughed more violently, emptying a mouthful of blood into his wineglass.

"What is going on?" one of the other men demanded.

Dr. Reiss remained eerily calm. "He told MI6 about our meeting," he explained. "That's why I changed our location."

Mr. Monza tried to defend himself, but could not. It was impossible to speak while he was coughing up bits of his own lungs into his napkin. The others stared at him in amazement. They'd thought he was one of them. How could he have given such information to the British Secret Service? And why?

"He was going to turn me in and then seek asylum from the West," Dr. Reiss continued, seemingly oblivious to the man slowly dying at the table.

"A smart man would have known I was on to him; would never have gotten on the plane," Dr. Reiss remarked as he grabbed Monza by his sweat-drenched neck and pushed his seat far against the wall. He stared into Monza's petrified eyes. "But I knew you would, because you actually thought you could fool me."

Mr. Monza coughed so hard his ribs began to crack.

"Those, gentlemen, are the sounds of a traitor!" Dr. Reiss shouted over the loud hacking.

The other men turned away, afraid to watch. But Reiss continued to stare into Monza's eyes. Clearly, the doctor was enjoying the show. It was, after all, of his own making. He wanted his to be the last face Mr. Monza saw.

Dr. Reiss smiled slightly as Monza's dead body slumped and fell from the chair. Then he turned to the others and spoke calmly, as though nothing had happened. "That was an accelerated form of Ebola," he explained. "It is the deadliest disease known to man. Highly contagious."

Suddenly a look of panic came over the five remaining men. Contagious!?

Dr. Reiss smiled at their reaction. It was exactly what he had expected. "But like all known diseases, there exist stockpiles of antiserum in the West, ready to stifle any outbreak."

A group of female attendants placed a single black pill in front of each man. Dr. Reiss stood and watched the men carefully. They were all painfully aware that Reiss himself did not have a pill. What did that mean? Was the pill truly an antidote? They looked over at Monza's lifeless, bloodstained body. The men realized they had no choice. Quickly each one swallowed his pill.

Reiss smiled at them and then took a pill as well. "Gentlemen," he continued calmly. "There's no antiserum for what I'm offering to you. No treatment, no protocol, no vaccine, no cure. The modern world has never seen anything like what I've uncovered."

"Uncovered?" one of the men asked.

"Yes, I branched out. Archaeology," Jonathan Reiss replied as he turned and headed back toward the curtain. But before he left the men alone, Dr. Reiss made sure to give the number for his private account in a Swiss bank. "Zero-seven-seven-four-four-six-eight-one. That is the account at Lardesbank in Bern. Nine figure deposit. A fair price for what you're getting. Those of you who pay will see their enemies eliminated. Those of you who don't, I hope none of your enemies buy it. You have twenty-four hours to decide."

It was several hours later when Dr. Reiss finally exited his aircraft. He was met at a small private airfield in Hong Kong, by his second in command, Sean. Sean was no stranger to danger—he'd formerly been with the Irish Republican Army and was now the man in charge of the day-to-day running of Dr. Reiss's operations.

A look of concern came over Dr. Reiss's face. Someone was missing from his welcoming party. Someone who'd had a very important assignment. "Where is Chen Lo?" Dr. Reiss demanded.

Sean handed his boss a fax. "He got the Orb, but MI6 is on to him. Rather than risk bringing the Orb here, he's waiting."

Reiss's eyes grew dark. "I just told a cabin full of men about Pandora; that clock can not be reset. Tell Chen Lo to bring the Orb at once."

CHAPTER FIVE

It didn't take Lara long to recuperate from her near-death experience in Greece. In fact, just a few hours later she was back at Croft Manor, her family mansion in the English countryside, practicing her stick-fighting technique—with the assistance of a slightly reluctant Hillary. For her part, Lara was dressed to kill—literally—in a tight, black fighting suit. Hillary, on the other hand, was dressed for fear—padded from head to toe to avoid any injury from Lara's well-pointed sticks.

The two battled back and forth like dueling knights, going from room to room. Eventually Lara was able to back Hillary into the library, where Bryce was busy downloading images from Lara's broken camera equipment.

"Bryce, what have you got?" Lara asked as she

leaped back to avoid Hillary's oncoming stick.

"I haven't even finished loading the images from your camera yet," Bryce replied.

That annoyed Lara. She whacked Hillary hard with a stick.

Hillary groaned and rolled his eyes toward Bryce. "Thanks," he moaned.

"What about references to the Orb?" Lara asked as she continued jabbing away at Hillary.

"I took the liberty of checking," Hillary replied as he ducked to avoid another blow. "Historical inventories of the Luna Temple do not list any Orb." *Smack*. He caught Lara with a hit to the side.

Lara raised an eyebrow appreciatively. That one wasn't bad. She lunged back at Hillary, eager for revenge. "Then I want both of you to make a list of every Orb mentioned in Greek history."

"Every one?" Bryce gulped.

"That's liable to be thousands," Hillary gasped, fending off Lara's continuing fencing assaults.

Finally Lara came in for the kill, whacking Hillary's stick from his hands. "Then we'll read thousands," she replied, driving her stick just past Hillary's ear. She flipped an especially thick book in the butler's direction. "You can start with that one," she told him.

* * *

While Hillary and Bryce searched through Lara's extensive library for information on ancient orbs, Lara was doing some more immediate research. She'd already called her old friend, Kosa Maasai, an ambassador at the British Embassy in Nairobi. Kosa was an expert in ancient artifacts, and Lara had a feeling he'd be the only one who could answer her questions about what she'd seen inside the Luna Temple.

Kosa stared at the fax in his hand and studied the petroglyphs Lara had photographed. It was a disturbing picture—an entire army, dead. And there in the middle of the fallen bodies was that small box Lara had noticed.

"What do you think?" she asked him over the phone.

"The symbols are a primitive version of Ol Maa," Kosa explained. "They read, 'With life comes death.' The figure on the floor is a Shadow Warrior, mythical creatures brought to the Earth by the gods to serve as Guardians."

"Guardians of what?"

Kosa didn't answer at first. "I don't know," he said finally, a note of distress in his usually jocular voice. "I'm sorry; that's all I recognize."

If Lara heard the apprehension in his tone, she didn't mention it. Instead she replied simply, "It's somewhere to start. Thank you, Kosa."

As Kosa hung up the phone, his face was washed with concern. His eyes were fixed on that horrifying image of death Lara had faxed to him.

Lara needed to think. And she thought best while horseback riding and target shooting. So she grabbed her rifle, went out to the stables, mounted her favorite horse, and went out to shoot a few terrorists. Well, not actual terrorists. More like cardboard cutout terrorists which Bryce had set up to pop out at her throughout the gardens at Croft Manor. It took a keen eye to blast away all of the cardboard killers, but Lara was up to the task.

At least until a helicopter began to fly overhead. The noise startled Lara's horse and made him buck, which threw Lara's aim off just enough to miss one of the cardboard cutouts. That absolutely infuriated her. Lara didn't like to lose—especially to a piece of cardboard. Angrily Lady Croft sped up, riding faster in the direction of the castle she called home. As she approached the doors, she threw her rifle over her shoulder, wrapped her shooting arm around her, and aimed backward at the target she'd missed. *Blam.* It fell to the ground with a thud.

Target shooting in the backyard. Just another relaxing afternoon at Croft Manor.

* * *

When Lara arrived back inside her mansion, she discovered two gentlemen in black suits and shiny shoes were waiting for her in the long hall. Hillary was already in butler mode, having brought in the tea service from the kitchen.

"Perhaps you gentlemen would like some tea while you wait?" he asked.

"No! They wouldn't," Lara answered for them as she burst into the room. "Tea is for guests. The door is for intruders."

"Lara," Bryce explained. "These men are from MI6."

"I know that, Bryce," she assured him with more than just a note of disdain in her voice. Lara had little use for members of the British secret spy organization. "It's clear from their soft hands and pressed suits that these are men who make decisions then leave the dirty work to others. I have no interest in . . ."

Before Lara could finish her tirade, one of the MI6 agents dropped a photo of Chen Lo on the table. The sight of the man who had killed her Greek friends stunned Lara.

"His name is Chen Lo," the agent informed her. "Along with his brother, Xien, he runs a ring of Chinese bandits known as the Shay-Ling. They deal guns, diamonds, antiquities . . . anything Chen Lo can sell on the black market. They followed you from the moment you arrived in Santorini."

"Why!?" Lara exclaimed.

"For this," the second agent replied, handing her a recreated fax of the Orb she had photographed in the Luna Temple. "After you were picked up at sea, a listening post in Malta intercepted the fax. It was sent from Chen Lo to a man named Jonathan Reiss."

"The scientist?" Lara asked. "Who won the Nobel Prize?"

The first agent nodded. "He's now the foremost designer of biological weapons in the world."

Lara's shock registered clearly on her face. Dr. Jonathan Reiss had always had a reputation for genius. Now he was using his genius for evil? It seemed impossible.

But of course, it wasn't. The MI6 agents proved that by handing Lara photos of Dr. Reiss's most recent work—the dead victims of his biological weaponry.

"His creations have been at the heart of every act of bioterror in the past fifteen years," one agent told her.

"Reiss's disdain for life is legendary," his partner concurred. "He has no political agenda, doesn't care who his weapons kill or why."

Lara's eyes fell on the photo taken in the Luna Temple. She focused on the drawing of the dead army and the mysterious box in the center of the picture. What was it Kosa had said the pictures meant . . . "With life, comes death"?

"We know Chen Lo followed you to obtain the Orb," the first agent continued. "We also know he'll deliver it to Reiss soon. What we don't know is why. Candidly that terrifies us. Reiss is not to be trifled with."

But Lara barely heard him. She was too focused on the pictures before her. And then it hit her. She knew exactly what Reiss was after. "Pandora's box!" she exclaimed suddenly. "That's why he wanted the Orb! He's going to use it to find Pandora's box!"

The agents exchanged looks. They seemed skeptical, at best.

"Do you mean the Greek myth?" one of them asked her. "Pandora is given a box by God, told not to open it. She does, and unleashes pain into the world?"

Lara fixed him with a steely stare. "I'm afraid that's the Sunday school version." She grabbed an antique globe from the table and pointed to a map of ancient Egypt. "How do you think life began? Shooting stars? Meteor? Primordial ooze? Well, in 2300 B.C., an Egyptian Pharaoh found a place he named the Cradle of Life where we— life—began. There he found a box. The box which brought life to Earth. The Pharaoh opened it, but all that was left inside was the Ramante—a plague which came as a companion to life."

Now the MI6 agents seemed completely confused.

36

"Companion?" they asked.

"In nature there's always a balance," Lara explained slowly. "The world comes in pairs. Right and wrong. Yin and Yang. What's pain without pleasure . . . ?"

"What did this plague do?" one of the agents demanded, eager to bring Lara back to the matter at hand.

"It leveled the Pharaoh's army," she replied simply.

The agents exchanged a second look. But this time they seemed more fearful than skeptical.

"The Pharaoh's son dispatched his finest soldier to take the box and transport it to the end of the world," Lara continued, spinning the globe until it stopped at India. "Two thousand years later, Alexander the Great reached India. His army was ravaged by a plague after one soldier discovered a small box among some remains."

"India," one of the agents mused. "That's where the Pharaoh's man brought it."

Lara nodded. "Alexander realized the box was too powerful to be trusted to any man, so he returned it to its home at the Cradle of Life. It's never been seen since."

"And this Cradle of Life is where?"

Lara sighed. "No one knows. Alexander found it using a map that was with the box. A map he then hid. The name he gave this map was Mati. A literal translation of the word *mati* is 'eye.'" She held up the picture of the Orb. Then, sensing that the agents still didn't get it, she added, "The Orb is the map, hidden in the Luna Temple by Alexander. Reiss will use it to find Pandora's box. When he does, when he opens the box, he'll unleash a weapon more terrible than any you can imagine."

Lara turned and led the men into her library, where she could better study the photographs she'd taken of the Orb. Bryce had been working on his computer and was able to use the photos to create a virtual 3-D version of the Orb.

"The marking are definitely a pattern," Bryce noted, "but even if I figure out what they represent, we won't be able to read the full map because we don't have a full view of it. . . . See?"

Lara studied the drawings. There were portions of the Orb's surface she had not had time to photograph. Still, they would have to make do with what they had. "Get to work on how to read it," she told Bryce. Turning to Hillary, she added, "I'll have to start packing."

As Lara turned to leave the room, the agents stopped her in her path. "On behalf of Her Majesty, we formally request you find and recover this box before Doctor Reiss."

Lara didn't even attempt to hide her amusement. "Now that I have permission," she said, laughing, "just tell me where to find the Orb."

"Last we heard, it was with Chen Lo and the Shay-Ling

somewhere in China," one of the agents informed her. "I'm afraid finding them will be next to impossible, but we'll assign you two of our best agents to help."

"I don't want them," Lara replied bluntly.

"With all due respect," the agent replied, "Archaeology doesn't qualify you—"

"I didn't say I don't need help," Lara assured him. "But your agents will never get me to Chen Lo in time. I need an insider. Someone who knows the Shay-Ling. Their methods, hideouts . . . I need Terry Sheridan."

The older of the two agents, Bryce, and Hillary were all aware of who Terry Sheridan was, and what dangers he posed to the world and to Lara herself. The younger agent, however, seemed not to have a clue.

"Not if he were the last man on Earth," the first agent informed her gruffly. He noted the perplexed look on his partner's face and explained, "Terry Sheridan, formerly a commander in the Royal Marines. Quite possibly the finest, most lethal soldier ever to serve this country, who one day, for reasons known only to him, disappeared. He resurfaced as a traitor. A mercenary selling his skills to the highest bidder. You don't expect me to put him on the trail of a weapon he'll turn around and auction?"

"I'm not any happier about the idea than you," Lara

told him. "But Terry is the only man I know who can get me to Chen Lo in time."

"Lady Croft, some men are capable of betraying their friends, but Terry Sheridan is the only one I know who enjoys it," the agent reminded her.

"Then it's lucky for us Terry's friends include Chen Lo and the Shay-Ling. . . . Isn't it?"

CHAPTER SIX

As Lara rode in a truck bound for Barla Kala prison in Kazakhstan, Hillary's words rang in her ears. "A leopard can't change his spots," he had warned her. Lara knew it was so. Terry Sheridan would always be the two-faced, dangerous man she had known in the past. But she needed his skills now. Working side by side with him was a risk she was going to have to take.

She leaped off the truck and walked bravely into the prison. It was like no other jail she'd ever seen. This converted Soviet missile silo was a place where only the most vicious, hardened criminals who were a danger to the planet were kept.

A smarmy, dark-haired man with a pair of headphones around his neck stepped out to greet her. "I am your host,

Armin Kal. Welcome to Fantasy Island." He laughed at his own joke.

The irony of his statement was not lost on Lara. Some fantasy. Prison guards were everywhere, armed with loaded AK-47s. Two men carried a dead body on a stretcher across the yard. This was no fantasy. This was a nightmare. A nightmare men like Terry Sheridan lived every day.

Lara walked beside Armin Kal as they crossed the prison yard and entered the main building. "We don't get visitors here," Armin said. He looked her over. "Not like you. You're very brave." He pulled the headphones over his ears.

"What are those for?" Lara asked.

"You." Armin Kal motioned to a guard. "Go ahead."

The guard released the remote lock, and Armin and Lara entered the cell block. Almost immediately the prisoners began shouting catcalls in her direction. It had been ages since they'd seen any woman, especially a woman with Lara's considerable physical charms.

Finally they came to the solitary confinement block. Four armed guards stood watch outside a small cell. Slowly Lara approached the door.

"I always knew one day you'd rescue me," Terry Sheridan said without even turning in Lara's direction. He didn't have to look. He knew his visitor was Lara. He could feel her energy in the air. He would recognize the sound of her footsteps anywhere. "Lara Croft," he greeted her.

"Hello, Terry."

"You're favoring a leg," he remarked, still refusing to turn around. "What happened?"

"Argument," Lara stated flatly. She looked down at the small cut on Terry's hand. "What happened to your hand?

"Argument," he replied.

"I'd hate to see the other bloke," Lara mused.

"Maybe you did," Terry replied. He turned to face her with more than just a touch of menace in his dark eyes. "They're offloading him now."

Lara stared at him. The dead body on the stretcher had been Terry's work.

Her surprise was not lost on Terry Sheridan. A thin smile came across his lips. The same smile that often lured his enemies into forgetting that this was a dangerous man who at any moment might strike like a cobra. "So, what do you think of the place?" he asked her finally. "Not quite Croft Manor . . ."

Lara dangled a set of keys from her hands, but said nothing.

"Key to your heart?" Terry asked mischievously.

Lara shook her head. "To a flat in Zurich. Or you can

pick another city if you want. Your record will be expunged, citizenship restored . . ."

"By?" Terry asked curiously.

"MI6."

"Would that make me Faust or the devil?" Terry asked.

"Pick," Lara replied. "They'll also arrange a new identity for you."

"You think I'd need their help?"

"Having two faces doesn't count," she assured him.

Terry stopped for a moment and studied Lara's face. "What do I have to do?" he asked her finally.

"There anything you wouldn't?" she snapped back.

"You like that about me." Terry smiled.

Lara wasn't about to play games with Terry Sheridan. "You have to take me to the Shay-Ling," she said, all business.

"The Shay-who?"

"Chen Lo took something from me. I want it back."

Terry studied her carefully. "You, or MI6?" He smiled slightly. "The Shay-Ling are hard to find. But you know that, or you wouldn't be here. . . ."

"The government will wire you five million pounds sterling when we succeed," Lara continued, eager to keep control of the situation squarely in her court. "Call it second-chance money."

"Or life insurance, for you," Terry countered.

"I don't need any," Lara assured him.

Terry stared at her and laughed. "You and I. Working alone."

"Easier to see through you that way," Lara told him pointedly.

"What happens afterward?" Terry asked. "When MI6 decides that me back in the world is not such a good idea."

"Then I'll feel sorry for whomever they send to get you," Lara answered.

"Who they send is not the point," Terry told her ominously. "It's you I'll hold responsible."

"Naturally."

Terry studied her face. He knew Lara well. She wouldn't be here if she didn't have an ace in her pocket. "You have authorization to kill me," he noted suddenly.

"Anytime, any reason."

Terry nodded. Suddenly it all made sense. "What is it they say, 'Hell hath no fury. . . ?'"

Now it was Lara's turn to laugh. Then, as if reconsidering her whole offer, Lara suddenly began to walk away. Out of the cell.

Out of his life.

"The Shay-Ling are ghosts, Croft," Terry called after her. "They move constantly. Their home is the most

45

remote region of mountains in China. Maybe on Earth."

"Region?" Lara answered, turning. "You'll have to do better than that."

Terry sighed. Obviously Lara was not going to change her mind. She would be in charge. If there were to be a deal at all it would be her way, or no way. "Get me into China," he said finally. "I'll get you to them in a day."

That was good enough for Lara. She nodded her head, and the guards opened Terry's cell door, then stepped aside, allowing Terry and Lara to pass. "No money, no guns, no weapons of any kind," Lara continued to lay out her conditions.

"Talk about taking the fun out of life," Terry moaned.

"Your only concern is Chen Lo," Lara reminded him. "Run, you'll be hunted. Give me trouble, you'll be back here. Are we clear?"

"Sure, Croft," he agreed. "You're in charge."

Armin Kal watched as Lara and Terry left the Barla Kala prison. The moment they were beyond the prison walls, he picked up his phone and dialed.

"I need to speak to Doctor Reiss," he hissed into the receiver. "Someone is looking for Chen Lo."

CHAPTER SEVEN

Within hours Lara and Terry found themselves in a quiet lakeside village in China. They'd arrived there in record time, courtesy of a stealth glider Lara had arranged. She'd programmed the plane to lead them into a nearby village to avoid being spotted by any Shay-Ling members. It was a plan Terry heartily agreed with—except for one detail. Now they would need transportation to get them through China. This village was far too rural to have the kind of vehicle they would need for a job like theirs. "Expecting to locate a vehicle in a place like this?" He shook his head. "You planned badly."

Lara didn't answer. Instead she spotted a pair of old horses grazing in a field. "How far do we have to go?" she asked him.

"Farther than that," Terry told her. He eyed Lara suspiciously. It was obvious to him that she knew something he didn't. There must be a form of transportation somewhere nearby that would get them to the Luoyang province, where the Shay-Ling often hid.

The question was, just where was this vehicle?

Terry walked over toward an abandoned truck. Hmmm. That looked good—until Terry realized the truck had no wheels.

Ignoring Lara's amusement Terry went off in search of another mode of transportation. Aha! From the corner of his eye he spotted a white canvas covering what looked to be a motorcycle. Triumphantly he whipped the canvas off . . . only to find a bicycle hidden underneath.

"I expected better, Croft," Terry said in a disparaging tone. "I expected much, much, better."

Lara didn't answer. Instead she entered a nearby farm, and approached a Chinese woman. She greeted her in Chinese and then hugged her tightly. This was not just any Chinese farmer. This was Shumei, one of Lara's most trusted allies. And this, Terry figured, was no farm.

"Everything ready?" Lara asked her.

The old woman nodded. "Your clothes and guns over there. Knives back there. And I took the liberty of tuning your bike."

Lara's face lit up like a child's on Christmas morning. "May I?" she asked, racing over to look at the remarkable spread of gadgets and gear Shumei had gathered for her.

As Lara eyed the weapons, Shumei eyed Terry. "So this is him," she said matter-of-factly. "Let's get you some gear."

Lara picked up her phone and dialed home. "It's me," she said as soon as Hillary answered on the other end.

"What is the happy couple up to?" Hillary asked, unwilling to hide his disdain for Terry and his disapproval of Lara's traveling alone with a man who was so dangerous—both to her life and to her heart.

"Accessorizing," Lara told him. "Where are we on reading the Orb?"

Immediately Hillary patched Lara's call through to Bryce, who at that very moment was in his trailer, busily flying a remote control helicopter around the room. The 3-D model of the Orb remained on his computer screen, but he hadn't been able to do much with it. "Maps have a key, Lara," he explained. "A legend, a scale, yes? The Orb's key is not on the Orb. It must have been lost—"

"Or was somewhere in the Temple," Lara interrupted. "Go through every image I took. Start with things near the Orb. The key would have been linked to it in some way."

Bryce sighed, and brought his helicopter in for a landing. It was time to go back to work. "Right."

Lara hung up the phone and walked over toward Terry and Shumei. Terry was now dressed and suited up with his travel equipment. Lara noted that the time in prison had not changed him at all. Terry looked remarkably like the same man she had known before he had gone to prison.

"It's not like Lara to take a partner," Shumei mused aloud. "Where are you two going?"

Terry flashed his signature grin. "Maybe a nice walk, fresh mountain air, stop by my friends the Shay-Ling and then play it by ear."

Shumei's face grew anxious at the sound of the word "Shay-Ling." Lara was involved in great danger. But she knew better than to say anything to Lara about it. Instead she led Lara and Terry to their motorcycles.

Terry studied his bike carefully. It was a nice motorcycle—sleek, shiny, and capable of going high speeds and long distances. But his bike was nothing compared to Lara's motorcycle. Judging by the spectacular size and make of her vehicle, there was no doubt Shumei knew who was the boss.

Lara knew it too. She smiled triumphantly at Terry.

"The Shay-Ling watch all the roads," Terry told her, trying to avoid her look. "We'll have to go around the back . . ."

Lara shook her head. "We'll go straight."

"Maybe you didn't hear me, Croft," Terry said. "They'll have men on every road from here to Luoyang."

Lara smiled knowingly. "Not every road," she assured him.

Lara was right. The Shay-Ling didn't have any henchmen lined up along the Great Wall of China, which was why Lara could safely drive straight across the top. Of course Terry's motorcycle wasn't quite as well equipped. He was forced to ride alongside the wall below her.

When they reached a quiet unpopulated area of the country, Terry stopped and dismounted from his bike. "From here it's by foot," he told her.

Lara stared at the sprawling hills before her. It seemed like a challenge to take on by foot. Still, if Terry could do it . . . Lara leaped off her bike and grabbed her backpack.

"Best to reconsider that no-gun rule," Terry said, testing her.

But Lara wasn't falling for his games. "No," she replied firmly as she trudged up toward the hills.

For a while the two traveled in silence, each keeping their eyes firmly pointed on the mountains ahead, searching for members of the Shay-Ling who could be hidden behind any tree. Finally, it was Terry who broke the silence.

"So where do I fit in?" he asked her.

"You're my guide. . . ." Lara began.

Terry shook his head. "I mean, when you think back on the vast scheme of your life, where do I fit in? Was I a bump in the road? The love of your life? Was I time well spent? Four months—more good than bad?"

Lara shot him a bemused look, but refused to answer. It was best to keep men like Terry Sheridan guessing.

CHAPTER EIGHT

Guessing games were also Jonathan Reiss's specialty. He had to keep his operations secret to maintain his diabolical business. And Reiss knew that the best way to keep a secret was to do it right out in the open. That explained the extremely public facade he'd given his lab.

To anyone passing by, the building looked like a crowded outdoor mall in Hong Kong. But the truth was this was anything but. In fact the mall was merely a front for Jonathan Reiss's laboratory. The place was filled with security cameras and guards, but very few men could make their way down to the Hot Zone, where the real biochemical work took place. In fact only Dr. Reiss, his associate Sean, and a few bodyguards had clearance to enter the basement area.

At the moment Dr. Reiss and Sean were in the Hot Zone meeting with a guest—the messenger sent to deliver the Orb. Unfortunately the messenger had not done his job. He'd made a delivery all right, but it was not the Orb. Inside his package was a cell phone, with a number already punched in.

"Is there anything you can tell me about this?" Dr. Reiss demanded of the messenger.

The man shook his head nervously. He knew nothing about the phone. He was just the messenger.

There's an expression that says "Don't shoot the messenger." But Dr. Reiss didn't live by that adage. In fact he was a believer in just the opposite. With a nod of his head, he ordered Sean to kill him.

As the messenger was dragged away, Dr. Reiss grabbed the phone and pushed the TALK button. Within seconds Chen Lo answered.

"I hope you didn't like your messenger," Jonathan Reiss told him.

"I didn't," Chen Lo replied. "But I did like the men I lost in the Temple."

"You underestimated Lady Croft," Jonathan Reiss told him bluntly.

"I underestimated how much this Orb is worth," Chen Lo countered.

As he spoke, Dr. Reiss flipped through his file on Chen Lo, stopping at a photograph of the gangster's wife and children. "There are so many horrible diseases," Jonathan Reiss mused in an ominous tone. "Things we are particularly susceptible to as children. You never know when you could find yourself holding little Shiho and Tai's hands as a mysterious ailment begins to ravage their bodies . . ."

Chen Lo laughed viciously. "You kill them, and I'll give your Orb to Lady Croft. My scouts tell me she's a few miles from here as we speak. I wonder how much she'd pay. . . ."

"I'll transfer an additional twelve million dollars to the twelve million currently awaiting release," Dr. Reiss assured him. "I will release it all once you've delivered the Orb. And Lady Croft's body."

That didn't seem too much to ask. "The Orb will come by truck to the Flower Pagoda in Shanghai, 9 P.M." Chen Lo assured him. "You'll find Croft's body with it." With that Chen Lo hung up on Dr. Reiss.

Almost immediately the Shay-Ling leader dialed a new number. When the party on the other line answered, Chen Lo gave his order. "Tell Xien to bring them in alive."

Terry and Lara were currently wandering around in what appeared to be the middle of nowhere. Although Terry seemed confident Lara wasn't so sure he knew where he was going. She studied his face as he surveyed the road ahead.

"You don't have any idea where they are, do you?" she asked him.

Terry shook his head. "You're impossible, you know that?"

"You pretended to know where they were so I'd get you out," Lara accused.

Terry grew angry. "This isn't some tomb, and the Shay-Ling aren't mummies," Terry reminded her. "They're killers. If you don't trust me . . ." He let his voice trail off.

Lara pulled out her gun and pointed it directly at him. "I'm sorry, but I don't have any time to waste," she told him.

Terry stared at the gun in her hand. "Normally you hand it to someone butt first," he joked, giving her a thin smile.

But Lara had been taken in by that look far too often. It wouldn't work on her anymore. She kept the gun pointed straight at him.

"Go ahead, pull the trigger," Terry said, his eyes staring at something behind Lara. "I'd rather you than them."

Lara turned around suddenly, and came face-to-face with eight vicious members of the Shay-Ling.

"So, Terry," the one they called Xien said. "What part of 'Never come back here' didn't you understand?"

Terry turned to Lara. "You wanted to find the Shay-Ling," he remarked in a dry tone.

Two members of the Shay-Ling grabbed Lara from behind and searched her, while two others took her guns and tied her arms in front of her.

"The only way we can get into their place is as prisoners, okay?" Terry told her.

"You might have told me that little gem before," Lara replied.

A member of the Shay-Ling shoved his booted foot in Terry's face and tied his arms together.

"Make Chen a better offer than his buyer," Terry said from beneath the man's foot. "He'll cross them."

"Even if his buyer is Jonathan Reiss?" Lara wondered.

Now it was Terry's turn to be surprised. "You might have told me that little gem before," he shot back.

Xien and his men dragged Lara and Terry up a steep hill at gunpoint. For the most part, the path was abandoned, although from time to time, Shay-Ling workers would carry coffins filled with stolen ancient artifacts down the path to the flatland below. It was obvious that the Shay-Ling had a very efficient operation.

After a tiring climb the prisoners were eventually led to the upper landing of the hill. There was nothing around other than armed guards—and a one-hundred-foot drop to the ground. No visible escape route.

Several Shay-Ling guards forced the duo into a cave. Xien observed them for a moment and then went off to report to Chen Lo.

"They put up a fight?" the Shay-Ling leader asked Xien.

"Didn't give them a chance," Xien replied. "Why?"

"Because Terry always has an angle, and if he didn't fight . . ." Chen Lo stopped to consider things for a moment. Finally he made his decision. "Get the Orb on the road to Shanghai," he ordered. "Reiss has doubled his price. I'm going to find out why."

As Chen and Xien spoke, Lara and Terry were having a private moment of their own—if you can consider being surrounded by Shay-Ling guards private.

"Bet I'm looking pretty good to you right now," Terry teased.

Lara scowled.

"Were you really going to shoot me?" he asked her.

"Oh I bet she would have," Chen Lo's deep, threatening voice interrupted. "I've seen her work first hand."

It took all of Lara's self-control to remain calm as she

came face-to-face with the man who had so savagely mur-
dered Gus and his two sons while leaving her for dead. She
watched as Chen Lo walked over toward Terry and patted
him on the back as though they were old chums.

"Did Terry tell you the last time any of us saw him, he
was riding away in a truck?" Chen Lo asked Lara. His
voice grew dark. "It was filled with Ming vases I found
near the Longmen Grottoes. And beside him was his baby
sister." Chen Lo indicated toward a gigantic, angry guard.

Terry gulped sheepishly. From the look on the guard's
face he still hadn't forgiven Terry for messing with his
sister.

Chen Lo turned and stared Terry down. "You shouldn't
have come here."

"It got me out of prison." Terry shrugged. "Besides, the
lady's got a good offer. Better than Reiss."

"Really," Chen Lo replied, trying to keep his curiosity
in check. "Should I take it?"

"Take it," Terry advised. "Or better yet, you and I ran-
som her and the thing back to the British for triple." For a
moment his words hung there in the air—cold, calculating,
and uncaring.

Chen Lo began to laugh. "Let's discuss it," he said.

Terry tried to stand, but Chen Lo stopped him in his
tracks. "Not you, Terry," he said. "Lady Croft and I. You

wait here and"—he turned to the gigantic, angry guard—
"catch up."

Another guard yanked Lara to her feet. She and Terry
had only a second before they were separated. "I'll need
three minutes," she told him.

Terry looked at his watch. "Terrific," he said, trying to
avoid the glare from the giant guard.

CHAPTER NINE

As Lara was led off, she noticed the medallion Chen Lo wore around his neck.

Chen Lo noticed her expression and held the medallion out so she could get a better look. "You remember it," he said. "I took it as a trophy."

"I'll have to do the same," Lara assured him.

Chen Lo looked at her appreciatively. He respected her attitude. "There's something else I think you'll appreciate," he said as they passed through a narrow opening in the cave and came to a section with a low ceiling. There were lights strung around the room. Lara gasped. It was filled with rows and rows of life-size terra-cotta warrior statues. It was a tomb raider's bounty like none she'd ever seen before.

"This is the largest group of terra-cotta warriors I've

found," Chen Lo boasted. "The King of Qin made them for use in the afterlife. To fend off enemies he made in this one."

Lara laughed. "You and I both need a set."

"I'd be happy to sell some to you," Chen Lo replied.

Lara was quiet for a moment. Finally she said, "I hope you are as entrepreneurial with the Orb."

Chen Lo looked at her, but said nothing.

"You lost men, I lost men," Lara reminded him. "I see no reason why we should both lose again."

"And if I want double what Reiss offered me?"

"If it's still here," Lara agreed.

"It's very valuable," Chen Lo remarked, in an obvious attempt to fish for information.

"If you knew that, you would also know Reiss will kill you the moment you give it to him," Lara advised.

"But your government will guarantee my safety?"

Lara shook her head. "I will."

"That must hurt. Saying that to me."

Lara swallowed hard. It did hurt. But she needed the Orb more than her pride. "Take the offer," she said.

Chen Lo laughed in her face "You presume to give me orders?"

"Take the offer," Lara repeated, "before it expires."

Chen Lo stared at her. He was no longer interested

in playing games with Lara Croft. "No thanks."

Lara shrugged. "Then I'll have to force you."

"Then I'll have to kill you."

Lara gave him an icy stare. "It's not going to be as easy as, say . . . killing innocent people from behind."

"Sure it is." Chen Lo smiled as brought his gun up and aimed it right at her.

Wham! Lara kicked it from his hand before his finger could hit the trigger. The gun flew across the floor. *Pow!* Lara landed a perfect sidekick to Chen Lo's side then spun a round and landed a flying sidekick to his head.

A lesser man would have fallen to the ground in pain. But not Chen Lo. He stood his ground, annoyed, but uninjured.

Both Lara and Chen Lo had the same thought. Both grabbed for an ancient spear from the rack of spears behind them. But Chen Lo was quicker than Lara. He kicked the rack from her grasp, sending the spears flying. Lara ducked to avoid being pierced by a flying blade.

Chen Lo also had a distinct advantage over Lara. Her hands were still bound together with heavy rope. His were free, and therefore, he was able to snatch a spear in midair. He wasted no time going after Lara, thrusting the spear straight for her. Lara, however, was quick and avoided his attack with rapid, catlike moves.

But she couldn't duck him forever. Even now, Chen Lo

had her backed into a corner with only five feet of space between her and the back wall of the cave. Lara's only hope for survival was to free her hands.

Chen Lo thrust his spear straight for Lara's stomach. She whirled around, bringing one leg over the oncoming spear, and cutting the rope that bound her hands on the point of the spear that was now between her legs. As her hands came free, Lara whirled around and kicked Chen Lo in the chest. Chen Lo retaliated with a powerful kick to Lara's face. She staggered back in pain.

It seemed that for once Lara Croft had met a foe worthy of her considerable skills. She would need all her wits to come out of this battle alive. Chen Lo could not be defeated by strength alone.

Lara took a deep breath and regained her balance. Then, as Chen Lo reached for another spear, Lara took advantage of his sudden switch in attention. She ran off and hid in a dark shadowy area, out of his sight. She stood there in the shadows as quiet as a mouse. Silence was more important than anything now. There were plenty of dark areas in the cave; shadows formed by giant statues. The trick was to slip around the room, hiding in the shadows, out of the sight of Chen Lo.

But Chen Lo was on to her. He stalked her like a leopard hunting his prey.

Crash! Lara jumped as a terra-cotta head exploded in

front of her. She spun around just in time to catch the sight of another giant warrior getting cut in half. Chen Lo was searching for her. Cutting his way through the shadows with his spear. Just as the shadows hid Lara, Chen Lo was taking advantage of their darkness as well. He was like a ghost; Lara knew he was there, but she couldn't see him anywhere.

An invisible enemy armed with spears. Could anything be more dangerous? *Slam!* One of the terra-cotta warriors fell to the ground, pinning Lara beneath it, and almost stabbing her with its stone sword. Quickly Lara rolled out from beneath the statue and leaped to her feet—just in time to see another ancient statue crash to the ground.

And then she saw Chen Lo standing just where the stone warrior had once stood. Like the ancient fighters he had a sword in his hands and was ready to pounce.

Lara whipped to the side, reached down, and managed to grab a spear of her own. Then she climbed up onto the head of one of the stone warriors. She leaped from statue to statue, landing precariously on their heads as Chen Lo pursued her from below. He chopped at the statues furiously, trying to get his hands on Lara.

Lara spied a string of lights just above her head. Quickly she whirled her spear around in the air, slicing right through the light bulbs. The glass bulbs shattered into a thousand splintered pieces. Some of those nasty shards landed on Chen Lo, slicing his face.

The pain distracted the Shay-Ling leader just long enough for Lara to run off toward a skinny, rickety bamboo ladder at the front end of the cave. She leaped for it. Unfortunately, the ladder was old, and the rungs crumbled under her weight.

Lara grabbed for the bamboo pole that remained. She studied it for a moment and then got an idea. The pole looked remarkably like the sticks she and Hillary had sparred with. She whirled around and faced Chen Lo. He was now coming at her with an amazing ferocity, like nothing she'd ever seen before. He no longer carried spears. Instead, he had machete-like swords in his hands.

Machetes versus a bamboo stick? Lara definitely didn't have the advantage, and Chen Lo knew it. With a single motion, he cut her pole in half—giving Lara two weapons.

But that was no help. Despite her best moves Lara was unable to keep Chen Lo at a distance. He sliced away at her sticks, breaking them into four pieces, then eight. Before long, her stick was sliced to bits.

Lara was desperate. Quickly she threw one of the sharpened pieces of bamboo toward Chen Lo. The stick pierced his skin and momentarily pinned his arm down. Blood began to run down his shirt. Now the warrior was in pain . . . and furious. He had no more patience. He was determined to finish off Lara Croft once and for all! He backed Lara up against a wall of crates and sent his blade smashing down.

Lara ducked at just the right moment and managed to dodge the blade by a millimeter. Instead of hitting Lara, the blade broke open the top of one of the crates. Inside was a pile of old rifles—303s with bayonets attached. Lara grabbed a rifle, fired straight for Chen Lo, and watched in horror as nothing happened.

There were no bullets in the gun! Quickly, Lara changed gears. Instead of shooting she used the rifle's bayonet, ramming it straight through Chen Lo's foot, and pinning him where he stood. He screamed in pain, and dropped his machete, as Lara used the butt of her rifle to force him to the ground.

"Where's the Orb?" she demanded of her captured prey. "Tell me, and it spares your life."

But Chen Lo didn't answer right away. His eyes drifted off toward an object in the distance. Lara rammed the rifle butt further into his chin.

"The Flower Pagoda," he said finally. "Shanghai. Nine P.M."

Lara smiled triumphantly and ripped the medallion from his neck. She fastened it around her neck and then, with contempt in her eyes, jammed the machete into the ground.

"We're even," she told him.

Just then the sound of guards rushing down the hall filled the room. The sudden noise distracted Lara for a moment . . . just long enough for Chen Lo to make a play for a gun on the floor. But before he could reach it, Lara got her bearings and threw his own machete at him.

The blade met its mark.

Lara's victory against Chen Lo was complete. The evil man would no longer be a danger to anyone.

But that didn't mean there wasn't any more danger to be met. Quickly Lara raced through the maze of broken terra-cotta warriors toward the front of the cave. There she spotted her own weapons being guarded by two of the largest men she'd ever seen. But Lara's adrenaline was still raging from her battle with Chen Lo. Her strength was almost super-human. Within seconds she'd knocked out both men and managed to grab back her own guns. Then, before leaving, she relieved one of the guards of his weapons as well.

Lara darted out of the cave and back up to the upper landing of the cliff. She was anxious to grab Terry and get away. But as she got closer she could hear the sounds of fighting, and screams of pain.

Obviously Lara wasn't the only visitor who'd been involved in battle. Terry had also been fighting off members of the Shay-Ling, particularly the giant who was fighting for his sister's honor. When Lara reached Terry, she found him on the ground, being kicked and punched by his guards. One of them spit in his face.

But Terry didn't flinch. In fact a beatific smile crept across his face. Out of the corner of his eye he could see that Lara had accomplished what she needed to do. He no longer had to keep this set of goons occupied and could now start fighting back.

Terry stood up, whirled around, and broke one guard's wrist with a single punch. He used his other fist to hit the other guard in the leg, shocking his femoral artery, and knocking him to the ground. The third guard, the giant, lunged at Terry. But Terry was quicker. A swift kick snapped the giant's kneecap, a punch punctured his lung. The giant fell to the ground with a thud.

Quickly, Lara threw a gun in Terry's direction. He looked at her curiously.

"I reconsidered!" Lara explained as she and Terry raced for a pair of hanging ropes that would lower them down off the cliff.

Bang! As the duo slid down the ropes headfirst, they shot up at the Shay-Ling, picking them off like ducks at a shooting gallery. *Bang, bang!* Terry felled two Shay-Ling guards near a truck. *Bang!* And then a third.

Bang, bang! Not to be outdone, Lara picked off two men at the top of the mountain, and then fired at the remaining men before hurtling toward the ground.

Lara and Terry leaped into an empty Shay-Ling truck and raced off, with Lara at the wheel. As Terry looked toward the back of the truck, making sure their getaway was clean, Lara used her cell phone to send a text message to Bryce.

F-O-U-N-D M-A-P K-E-Y

Terry turned around. "We lost them," he assured her as he checked his gun. There were still a few bullets left. He turned to Lara. "You said get you to Chen Lo, and I did. For me this is over."

"Of course it is," Lara agreed. She braked the Jeep to a stop and unlocked the door for him.

But Terry didn't budge. Instead he studied her face. "Tell me what this is about. Tell me what you're looking for, or where it is. Do that, trust me, and I'll help."

Lara shot him one of her steely stares. "I'll be fine. Thank you."

They exchanged glances, both knowing there was

nothing more to be said. Terry got out of the Jeep and shut the door. Lara watched as he walked slowly down the road. Logic wrestled with her emotions. She hoped she could live with the compromise she was about to make.

Finally, she put her foot on the gas and drove up beside him. "We need to be in Shanghai by twenty-one hundred," she told him matter-of-factly.

Terry shot her a grin. "I knew you'd miss me," he teased as he climbed back into the Shay-Ling's Jeep.

CHAPTER TEN

The roads to Shanghai were busy that day. Not only were Lara and Terry on their way to the city, but Xien was on his way there as well. As Xien drove along, his cell phone rang. He answered the call, his face falling, as his fellow Shay-Ling warrior told him the news of Chen Lo's demise.

"How did it happen?" he demanded. Then a look of anger and desire for revenge came over him. "Don't worry, I'll find her!"

Xien was not the only one to learn of Lara's victory over Chen Lo. Word had reached Dr. Jonathan Reiss as well. Unlike Xien, Reiss felt nothing about the death of the Shay-Ling leader. His mind was somewhere else completely. "Did she get the Orb?" he demanded of Sean as the two men boarded his helicopter.

Sean shook his head. "No. Xien has it," he assured his boss. "He's on his way to Shanghai. My guess is Croft is too. We have to change the location."

"No."

Sean seemed confused. "But if she comes to Shanghai . . ."

"Oh there's no 'if,'" Dr. Reiss assured him. "Croft will be there waiting for us . . . so we will be waiting for her." A diabolical grin lit up his face as he closed the door to his helicopter and sped off toward Shanghai.

Dr. Reiss knew how Lara's mind worked. And she did not disappoint. By the time Xien arrived at the Flower Pagoda in Shanghai, Lara was already busy, surveying the scene from the rooftop of a nearby fish shop, with Terry at her side. From that vantage point they could see Xien's truck as well as several mysterious black Mercedes all filled with Dr. Reiss's personal warriors.

"Seems like old times," Terry mused.

"Thirty, forty, against two," Lara said, sighing.

"Just once I'd like to go somewhere with you where there weren't people trying to kill us," Terry said.

Lara smiled a bit, despite herself.

"That's the first time you've smiled because of me," said Terry.

Lara stared at him. He seemed more relaxed than before—almost normal. "Why'd you do it, Terry? How does someone wake up one day and leave everything they've worked for?" She stopped for a moment and looked knowingly into his eyes. "They offered you a command. . . ."

"They offered me a desk," he countered. "A nice cozy office. A nice cozy life."

"All you had to say was no."

Terry shook his head. "By then I'd started thinking. I was tired of doing things somebody else's way. And it was always going to be someone else's way."

Lara frowned. It wasn't impossible for her to see how Terry must have felt. A man of his talent, his brains, his sense of adventure, to be chained to a desk. The frustration must have been unbearable. It would have challenged anyone's loyalties. And yet . . . "But deserting your men, your country," Lara argued.

"I've paid my price for that," Terry began. "I don't know what it says about me, but leaving my men, my country, didn't hurt as much as I thought. Leaving you was what did. You're a hard act to follow, Croft." Terry turned to look at her.

"The reason you and I got along? We both despise being normal. We both love what we do too much to leave room for much else. We're two of a kind, you and me."

"Terry, we're nothing alike," Lara assured him quietly.

Terry leaned toward her. "I don't think we're alike. I think we're a pair," he told her. His voice grew soft and intimate. "Opposite. Alone." He moved closer to Lara. She could feel his breath on her face.

Just then a helicopter whirred overhead. Reiss had arrived. Lara snapped to attention.

Just as Lara was aware of Reiss's arrival, the doctor was equally certain that Lara was waiting for him.

"She'll be somewhere with a vantage point of the helipad," Sean told him.

Dr. Reiss nodded and picked up his cell phone to call Xien. "My men have the landing pad covered," he reported.

"Why don't you set down in the square instead?" Xien suggested. "That way my men will also have things covered."

"Fine," Dr. Reiss agreed. "And in case you weren't aware, Croft is here."

"Oh, I'm aware," Xien assured him. He hung up the phone, got out of his truck, and headed toward the square to await the arrival of Reiss's helicopter. Behind him walked a man with a crate that was secured by a cloth strap. Inside it was the Orb.

From her vantage point on the roof of the fish shop, Lara scanned the skies, waiting for the helicopter to land. But when the helicopter made a sharp turn, Lara was caught by surprise. "They're not landing on the helipad!" she shouted to Terry.

Lara was on the move at once, scurrying across the rooftop. The roof was peppered with billboards and neon signs, with no visible way to get down to street level without being killed by one of Reiss's men or a member of the Shay-Ling.

"Croft," Terry called. He pointed toward a neon dragon sign. Lara grinned. Perfect. Quickly she kicked her pack over to Terry. He was going to need it more than she.

"See you over there!" Terry shouted as he watched Lara grab an extra bit of chain from the fire escape, and drape it over the cable holding the neon dragon. The cable stretched straight across the square. It was perfect—a zip line leading directly to where the helicopter was heading. In a single motion she held tight to the cable and pushed off from the roof.

As Lara flew overhead along the cable, Xien followed

Lara Croft is always game for water sports.

Bryce and Hillary, Lara Croft's two trusted companions

Lara Croft fears nothing.

Chen Lo meets
his match

Lara Croft fights to keep the Cradle of Life safe.

The ball is in Dr. Jonathan Reiss's court now. . . .

a similar path on the ground. He didn't even notice Lara soaring overhead—he was in too much of a hurry to greet Dr. Reiss. But just as the door of the helicopter opened, both Xien and Dr. Reiss spotted Lara. It was hard to miss her, arriving as she did on the neck of a dragon with her guns blazing.

Lara's firepower hit its mark, pummeling Reiss's helicopter with bullets. But as the neon dragon zipped past the helicopter it came too close to the whirring blades. In a single swipe, the chopper's main rotor decapitated the dragon—and threatened to do the same to Lara. She ducked in the nick of time.

There was no way Jonathan Reiss was going to let Lady Croft interrupt his business exchange. "Get us out of here!" he shouted to the pilot. Immediately the helicopter rose off the ground, moving straight up and ripping out part of a balcony above.

Before the helicopter reached its peak elevation Sean took a flying leap back down to the square—with his briefcase of money in hand. Then he and Xien began shooting at Lara, trying to finish her off once and for all before she could even reach the ground.

Xien and Sean weren't the only ones firing. While Lara ducked to avoid being hit by bullets from below, a shower of bullets was falling from above as well. But those bullets were designed to give Lara protection: They were coming from Terry's gun. He was jumping from roof to balcony around the square, covering Lara's moves and shooting the enemy before they could shoot Lara.

Lara smiled to herself. Deciding to give Terry a weapon had turned out to be a smart decision. But there was little time to congratulate herself. Already the headless dragon was threatening to burst into flames. Quickly Lara leaped from the dragon to another sign. She got off just in time to see the dragon sign explode, taking out a first floor fire escape as it slammed to the ground.

Lara leaped down from her sign and watched as a black Mercedes sped into the square. A door opened and Sean leaped into the car. Lara raced after the Mercedes, her arm raised as though she were about to fire. But Lara didn't shoot. Instead she leaped onto the car and using it as a ramp, swung her way onto the first floor of the next building. She was out of reach of Sean's gunfire, if only for a moment.

She hid in the building, quietly watching as Sean deployed his men to where Lara was last seen.

"We have her surrounded," Sean radioed Reiss, who was safely aboard his helicopter. "We're moving in."

"Keep her pinned. I'll get the Orb," Dr. Reiss radioed back. He picked up his cell phone and dialed Xien.

"We tried it your way," Reiss told Xien impatiently as

he eyed the Flower Pagoda. There was a moment of quiet in the square just before Reiss's helicopter took off.

Meanwhile Sean's men scattered around the building where Lara was last seen. She saw the men coming but stayed focused on looking for Xien and the crate containing the Orb. Xien's men approached the building from another angle and kept a sharp eye out for Terry.

While looking down at the square, Lara caught sight of Xien carrying the Orb crate toward the Flower Pagoda. She also spotted Terry hiding in the shadows.

Terry had safely avoided the earlier gunfire and gotten into a doorway. From his vantage point he saw Reiss's helicopter take off and instinctively knew, at the same time that Lara did, that Reiss and Xien were going to make the exchange at the Flower Pagoda.

Both Lara and Terry looked for a way to reach the Flower Pagoda in time to stop the transaction. Their eyes locked on the helipad. It might be close enough for Lara to get across, somehow.

"That's crazy," Terry muttered to himself, sensing Lara's plan. Sean's men and members of the Shay-Ling surrounded the entire structure. Getting to the Pagoda was nearly impossible.

"Perfect," Lara said with a smile. She looked down at Terry. It was now or never.

"This better be worth more than a few million," Terry said to himself as they both sprang into action.

Lara leaped up and grabbed a fire escape. Terry brought up the rear and covered Lara with gunfire. Together they heaved themselves up onto a neon sign above and climbed toward a balcony on the next building. They leaped from sign to sign, inching their way through a maze of neon, metal, and concrete, until they were directly below the roof of the helipad building.

"While I have you, I'd like to renegotiate my share," Terry said casually as they evaded the gunfire around them.

The two glanced at a large gap between their building and the Flower Pagoda.

"Sounds like you think we'll live," Lara said, surveying the situation.

"I don't, but just in case. Triple?"

"And here I thought you were going to ask me for my undying love and affection." Lara hoisted herself onto the helipad roof.

"That's what got me into this in the first place," Terry said to himself as he did his best to distract Reiss's men and to cover Lara. He climbed out onto the building's fire escape, but the ladder flipped around and fell onto the balcony of a nearby building. Luckily, Terry caught himself just inches before he hit the ground head first.

Lara was on her own on the helipad. She saw Xien approach Reiss's helicopter at the Pagoda and knew she had to act quickly. That's when she spotted a bamboo pole that had once been used for scaffolding.

She eyed the gap between herself and the Flower Pagoda and checked out the length of the bamboo pole.

"Not long enough. . . Oh well." Lara took a running start to the edge of the roof, planted the pole, and vaulted over the distance.

Reiss and Xien were about to make the exchange when they saw Lara in midvault, flying toward them. Instinctively Xien pointed his gun at Lara. But Reiss coolly aimed at Xien.

"Regards to your brother," Reiss said as he pulled the trigger. Now that he had the Orb he had no need for his partner in crime. At that moment Lara landed just beneath the helicopter's main rotor. Close call! The rotor chewed up Lara's bamboo pole into little splinters.

Reiss's helicopter began to rise as Reiss desperately grabbed for the crate containing the Orb. He began to pull it up into the helicopter, but Lara was quick. She sprang into action and grabbed a rope that was attached to the bottom of the crate. She held on as the helicopter ascended. It looked as if she had a good grip, but Reiss had the advantage—a gun, pointed right at her.

Lara pulled something out of her wristwatch and smacked her hand against the side of the crate; then she let go. This was one battle she could not win. There was no point in losing her life as well.

She fell onto the tiled roof of the Pagoda. She slid down the roof, and just as she was about to go over the edge, Lara propelled herself into a gymnastic flip, changing the course of her descent. She tumbled quickly toward the square, finally landing safely on her intended target—the canvas top of Xien's truck.

While Reiss's helicopter sped across the square he radioed Sean to let him know Lara's whereabouts. "They're all yours," he told Sean.

Sean immediately gave the order to block all the alleys. He would not let them escape again.

Lara scrambled to the back of the truck and cautiously opened the door. Seeing someone inside, she quickly drew her gun and prepared to fire.

"I'm getting tired of you pointing that thing at me," Terry said smugly.

Lara and Terry took cover behind the truck. The windows shattered from gunfire. Things didn't look good.

"There goes your Orb," Terry said. "Do you have any idea where he's going?" Lara and Terry ducked bullets whizzing over their heads.

"No. But I will. I put a TRACER on the crate." She pulled out her GPS and looked at the moving signal. "I don't go vaulting into thin air without a plan."

"Got a plan to get us out of here?" he asked, knowing that Lara Croft always had a plan.

"Bull," she remarked under her breath.

"Of course it's bull, they've got more men than we have bullets!"

Lara grinned. "No . . . bull," she repeated, pointing to an animal pen that was adjacent to the square. There in the middle of the pen were several angry bulls.

Terry shook his head. She must be crazy.

Sean and his men sat blocking a nearby alley, waiting for any sign of Lara and Terry.

"There!" Sean shouted to his men as he saw Lara and Terry heading for the bullpen.

Lara had to act fast. She quickly whipped off her jacket and turned it inside out. The lining was red—just what the bull had ordered! Lara waved her jacket and the bull leaped into motion. As the bull rushed past, Lara pulled herself onto its back and rode it out of the pen. Terry ran among the other bulls right alongside Lara and rapidly fired at Sean and his men. The rain of bullets was so heavy that Sean retreated into his Mercedes.

To escape Lara would have to get past that car. She

rode the bull at top speed toward the Mercedes and smashed it out of her way. Before Sean and his men knew what hit them, Lara and Terry were already gone.

Once they were safe, Lara checked the Orb's signal on her GPS, which was tracking the helicopter's course.

Jonathan Reiss was heading straight for Hong Kong.

A mad doctor with the means to destroy millions of people headed for a densely populated city.

Lara needed to find him and fast!

CHAPTER ELEVEN

Not long after leaving the square in Shanghai, Jonathan Reiss was back in his lab with Sean by his side. The doctor could barely contain his excitement as he watched the Orb being lifted from the crate by a pair of robotic hands inside the specially designed, secured Plexiglas chamber. Every precaution was being taken to keep the luminescent object safe.

"There was always a part of me that allowed for the possibility that Pandora's box was just a legend," Dr. Reiss admitted to Sean. "But seeing this, I know it's there."

Together the two men watched as a laser scanned every inch of the Orb's surface, mapping out each marking. When the procedure was well underway, Reiss turned to

Sean. "She escaped?" he asked, focusing his attention on the one person who stood in the way of his plan.

Sean nodded. "She has no idea where we are," he assured his boss.

"I'm taking no chances," Reiss replied. "Start transferring everything we need to manufacture an antidote to the jet."

Reiss's paranoia was not without reason. Lara did have an idea where they were. And at that very moment, she and Terry were onboard a hydrofoil, heading across the water to Hong Kong.

As Lara studied her GPS, keeping track of the Orb's every move, Terry went for breakfast. He returned with a scone and some tea, and watched Lara as she ate. There were plenty of people on the hydrofoil that morning, but Terry didn't see them. At that moment there was only Lara.

"We did well back there, Croft," he said quietly.

"Reiss has hours on us now," Lara said, remaining strictly businesslike.

Terry sighed. "You're welcome," he muttered sarcastically. "For saving you."

Lara didn't answer. She just stared at her GPS.

A few minutes later, Lara and Terry found themselves making their way through the crowded streets of Hong Kong.

The city was teeming with people. As the GPS directed them to a plaza filled with office buildings and skyscrapers, Lara seemed slightly bewildered. Was it possible Reiss's headquarters was hidden here?

"A weapons lab in the middle of the city?" Terry wondered, putting words to Lara's thoughts. "No way. He must have dumped the crate."

Lara checked her GPS and stopped. This was the place.

"In one of the buildings?" he asked.

"No," Lara told him. "It's exactly where we're standing."

Terry looked around. They were standing in the middle of the plaza, outside a mall. But they might as well have been in the middle of nowhere. The place where Lara and Terry were standing was a completely empty. There was no lab in sight. "Like I said, he dumped it," Terry insisted.

"No, he didn't," Lara argued, staring into one of the buildings.

Terry followed her gaze. An escalator in the lobby was going down to the underground mall. He and Lara looked at the street below their feet. Reiss's lab was just beneath them.

But Lara wasn't quite ready to rush into the lab. There was still one more thing she had to do before she grabbed the Orb from Reiss. She found a bank of pay phones and called home.

"Are you all right?" Bryce and Hillary demanded in unison as they hit the speaker phone in Bryce's trailer. He didn't need to ask who was calling. Lara was the only one who had the number.

"I'm in Hong Kong," she informed them. "I need you both to look at something." Quickly Lara attached a wireless Digi-cam to her belt.

Bryce and Hillary gathered around the computer monitor in the trailer and studied the picture Lara was now broadcasting to them. The medallion she'd won back from Chen Lo appeared on the screen.

"This was in the Luna Temple, close to the Orb," Lara explained. "I'm betting it's the key to reading those markings."

Bryce studied the picture of the figure playing a musical instrument. "Sound!" he exclaimed. "Brilliant."

As Bryce and Hillary conferred with Lara, Terry was busy making a call of his own. "I need an out for two people, midcity," he said into the phone. He waited a beat while the person on the other end responded. "Are you crazy?" he demanded, his face getting red. "How many times have you used it?" He waited another beat. "What do you mean, 'none'?" he demanded. Then, after considering his options, he added, "If that's the only way, then set it up."

Terry and Lara hung up their phones at almost the same moment. "Are we set?" she asked him.

"Piece of cake," Terry replied, although his voice didn't sound quite as confident as his words.

Lara and Terry waited until sunset to make their move. They mingled with the others in the square, and were able to move with shoppers unnoticed onto the down escalator. Before long they'd entered the underground world that housed Dr. Reiss's lab in an inconspicuous, unopened storefront. And it was none too soon. Reiss was already preparing to get the Orb away and out of danger as soon as the computer had finished scanning the information engraved on its surface.

"The jet is ready," Sean informed him as the two men stood alone in the room with the Orb.

Reiss nodded. "Call me with the location of the box as soon as you get it. Until then, make sure the Orb is never left unattended."

Reiss walked confidently from the lab into an elevator that would take him to the surface. He smiled slightly. His plan was now in gear. There would be no stopping them.

Or would there?

At that very moment Jonathan Reiss's worst nightmare—in the form of Lara Croft—had located the Hot

Zone, where the Orb was currently being housed. Of course Reiss had no idea that Lara had tracked him down so quickly.

For Lara, tracking down Reiss had been the easy part. The hard job lay ahead of her. It wasn't as though she could just stroll right in and take the Orb. Security guards sat at a desk watching the whole lab on a series of monitors. They would have to be dealt with first.

As soon as the guards spotted Lara and Terry in the security room, they reached for the alarm. But Lara was fast. She knocked two of the men out cold. Terry took care of the third.

Lara knew that she and Terry were going to have to split up. She would go for the Orb while he stayed here at the desk keeping watch. Somehow they would have to be able to communicate. But how?

Quickly she grabbed the walkie-talkie headset from one of the unconscious guards. After checking the frequency so that it matched her own headset, she handed it to Terry.

One problem solved.

Terry looked at the monitors and tried to study the layout of the lab. This was no straightforward path, though. Rather the interior of the lab was a maze filled with small, interconnecting rooms. It was going to be nearly impossible to find the Orb in a setup like this. Kind of like finding a needle in a haystack.

Of course needles in haystacks just happened to be one of Lara Croft's specialties. "What's that?" she asked, using the monitor controls to zoom in on an image that was currently being displayed on a computer screen. Some sort of writing or something. Lara was sure she'd seen it someplace before. . . .

The Orb! That was an enlarged image of what had been engraved on the Orb! In a flash Lara raced out of the room and headed toward the sterile room where Reiss's computers were scanning the engravings.

Carefully Lara slipped through a side door, leaving Terry to stand guard at the monitors, keeping an eye out for danger. As Lara made her way into the Hot Zone, she looked around. There were many people milling around in the hallway, all dressed in identical biohazard suits. So many people around would make it more difficult to get to the Orb.

"You've got to get everyone out," Terry whispered into his microphone.

"What do you suggest?" she whispered sarcastically into her headpiece. "The fire alarm?"

Actually that wasn't such a bad idea. Lara grinned to herself as she spotted a biohazard symbol on a glass door.

All she had to do was make people believe that a bio-hazardous substance had leaked into the air.

Quickly she took a tiny lab knife and punctured a small hole in a layer of the glass. The hole was barely visible, but it was big enough to set off the emergency evacuation system in the lab. Computer screens began to flash wildly: Security Breach! Evacuate Immediately!

"Not bad," Terry congratulated her. "But that's only the outer glass. There's no danger."

"Think anyone is paid enough to take that chance?" Lara whispered back into her walkie-talkie.

Lara had figured correctly. The lab technicians weren't about to wait around to find out if this had been a false alarm. They headed straight for the emergency exit and never looked back.

But as one of the men guarding the Orb turned to join the mass exodus, Sean waved his gun in his face. "Don't even think about it," he ordered in his thick Irish accent.

The man had little choice. It was either death from bio-hazardous materials, or death from Sean's gun. At the moment Sean seemed to be the more ominous of the two.

Sean looked around the room. "It's her," he said to himself, sensing that Lara was the cause of the commotion. Quickly he picked up his cell phone and dialed Jonathan Reiss's personal number.

Dr. Reiss picked up his phone as soon as it rang. But he couldn't hear anyone speaking on the other end. All he could hear were the alarms ringing all over his lab. Instinctively Dr. Reiss knew at once that Lara Croft had somehow discovered its location. He quickly turned back.

In the meantime Lara had made her way into the Hot Zone. She slid behind a counter and began to plan her assault on the Orb room. But Lara's plans didn't get very far. A guard surprised her from behind and held her tight as she struggled against his grip.

Suddenly shots rang out.

CHAPTER TWELVE

With a single burst of energy Lara broke free of the guard's grip and dove out of the way of the flying bullets. The guard was not as quick. The bullets meant for Lara pierced him instead.

Sean was not all that upset about losing a man, but he was determined to get Lara. He knew that wasn't going to be easy. Sean was well aware that it would take more than a few bullets to kill Lara Croft. It would take brains. Sean would have to trick Lara into coming into his field of fire. He pulled a second gun from his holster and quietly readied it on the spot. Then he ejected the clip from his first gun. Lara, hearing the empty clip, leaped out, ready to fire.

Just as Sean had hoped.

Blam! Sean fired off a round of bullets. She ducked

behind a counter. The bullets hit the counter, a back wall, and one poor lingering technician, who hadn't yet evacuated the building. Strangely he didn't seem the least bit upset that he'd missed Lara. In fact he seemed to welcome the challenge.

"I'm glad," he called out to her. "That would have been too easy." He pulled out his gun and blasted away at the counter behind which Lara was hiding. He listened for a moment for any sounds of life.

And then the lights went out.

Sean was totally confused. Obviously there was someone else in the building. The question was, who? Was it Dr. Reiss, a lab technician, or someone else; someone Lara had brought along for the ride?

Lara knew the answer to that one. She was pretty certain that Terry had killed the power in the room, in order to make it more difficult for Sean to find Lara.

But the darkness only seemed to make the hunt more interesting for Sean. The Irishman stood for a moment, listening. The room was quiet. The only sound was the hum of the computer systems. Still, instinctively, Sean knew Lara Croft was still alive.

"I'm waiting, Lara," he called out into the darkness as he trained his gun on the counter behind which he believed she still was hiding.

But Lara was no longer behind the counter. She'd moved to the shelter of a nearby desk. She crouched behind the desk and looked around to acclimate herself to her surroundings. As she searched the room, Lara suddenly noticed that it had mirrored ceilings.

Lara grinned. That would do quite nicely. She pulled out her guns and shot wildly at the mirrors. *Crash!* A huge section of the ceiling fell, and shards of glass rained down on Sean. Somehow he managed to dive out of the way.

The first time anyway. Lara immediately shot out the rest of the ceiling. There was another rainstorm of glass. Sean dove again, and while he managed to avoid the glass, he could not avoid Lara's elbow, which pounded him right in the head. Sean dropped to the floor, out like a light.

"Be careful what you wish for," Lara said, laughing as she stood and looked around. Her eyes fell on the computer that was scanning the Orb for information. According to the computer, the laser scan was already ninety-six percent complete, and climbing.

"I'm going off line," she whispered to Terry.

Terry understood. With a flick of the switch he turned the building's power back on.

Lara quickly wired up her ear-cam and immediately began to transmit information back to Bryce's trailer on the grounds of Croft Manor.

Within seconds she heard the voices of her two most trusted friends.

"Lara!" they exclaimed simultaneously, each sounding relieved to have heard from her.

"You understood the medallion?" Lara asked. There was no time for pleasantries.

"Yes," Bryce assured her. "The markings are sound waves. We've translated all the markings we could see on your images, roughly half the Orb."

Lara nodded. That was all she'd been able to photograph from inside the Luna Temple before Chen Lo had appeared. "Let's finish the set," Lara said, readying her handy Digi-cam. "I'll record the rest of the images, then send them to you. Once you have them, finish the translation and transmit the sounds back to me." She began to circle the Orb, transmitting images back to her friends.

As Lara transmitted the images of the Orb back to England, Terry kept his eyes on the images on the security monitors. His heart jumped as he noticed a tall man enter the building, followed by a huge muscleman.

Reiss and one of his bodyguards had re-entered the mall! They were heading toward the Orb room at a rapid pace. Terry had to warn Lara.

As Reiss and his guard entered the lab area, they stopped at the security station where Terry had been waiting, unbeknownst to them. Terry was hiding in the shadows as the two men checked the monitors. He watched as Reiss stopped the guard from sounding an intruder alert alarm. Obviously Reiss felt surprising Lara would be to his advantage.

Terry raised his gun. He had a partially blocked shot at Reiss, but he could make it. He aimed his gun carefully, and then lowered it again, refusing for some reason to take the shot. Dr. Reiss was free to walk through his lab, in search of Lara.

As he neared the Hot Zone, Reiss noted the small hole Lara made in the glass. It confirmed exactly what kind of opponent he was dealing with. "Smart girl," the doctor murmured quietly to himself.

At that very moment that "smart girl" was finishing photographing the Orb, and was about to complete the transmission of information back to Bryce and Hillary. But before she could pull the flash card out of her Digi-cam, she saw two reflections in the shiny surface of the Orb. Someone had entered the room!

Quickly Lara pocketed the camera. Then in a blur she spun around and fired off a round of shots. Surprisingly she didn't shoot at the intruders. Instead she took aim at the three computers that were decoding the information on the Orb, shooting out the first two with no problem. But before she could destroy the third computer, someone grabbed her from behind and slammed her head against the desk.

Lara should have killed Sean when she had the chance. Now he was awake, angry, and ready to exact his revenge. He placed the cold steel of his gun against her neck. She could hear his angry breathing in her ear as he prepared to shoot.

But Sean didn't shoot Lara right away. Instead he pocketed the gun and took a knife to her throat. He pushed her head down against the desk and with his free hand, bent her arm behind her. Why waste an opportunity for a little fun? Sean smiled. Clearly this was the kind of entertainment he enjoyed most.

But his fun was halted by Dr. Reiss, who entered the room and glanced at the one remaining computer. The progress monitor read 96 percent. "Not until we're sure the computer has done its job," he ordered Sean.

Reiss came around and stood in front of Lara, but his eyes never left the computer screen. Not even as he spoke directly to her. "When I was seven we moved to Calcutta," he recalled. "Filthy place. It was there I heard the local legend of a box that purged Alexander of half his army. I filed it away in the back of my mind."

"You really believe you'll be able to control what's in the box?" Lara interrupted, baiting him. "Make it another of your weapons?"

Now Reiss stared at her, amazed that she could even ask such a question. "Really, Lara, you disappoint me." He turned to the bodyguard who'd accompanied him back into the building. "Have we received payment from all the buyers?" he asked.

The man nodded.

At first Lara seemed confused. Then she raised her eyes high enough to see a map of the world on the wall. Bright red circles indicated the location of each of Dr. Reiss's clients. They were in every corner of the world. A sickening feeling came over Lara as she realized what Dr. Reiss had in mind. "You don't want to control it!" she exclaimed.

Jonathan Reiss smiled, but said nothing.

"You're using the buyers," Lara continued. "They release what you give them, thinking it's just another weapon. Then the world blames them for what happens."

Jonathan Reiss stared into her eyes. "What's left of the world blames them," he corrected her. He glanced at the monitor. Ninety-eight percent complete. It wouldn't be long now.

"Politics bores me," he continued. "One side killing

another over some god or some resource like oil. Trivial compared to the real challenge we as a species face. Look around and you'll see it, Lara. The human race is growing weak."

Lara shot him a look of disdain, but Dr. Reiss ignored her. Instead he continued his theory on humanity. "I grew up on a farm," he explained. "On a farm when the herd is at risk from disease, or has simply grown too fat and frail for its own good, you thin the herd. That's what the box is for—to weed out our weak, our feeble. Those races which would have expired but for our ludicrous notion that all men are created equal, that we should help our weaker members to survive. Every organism has a state of balance, mankind is out of ours. Properly thinned, we'll grow and evolve." He glanced at the progress monitor again. Ninety-nine percent.

"You're insane!" Lara exclaimed.

"I'll make enough antiserum to spare the best and brightest," Dr. Reiss continued. "Heads of corporations, heads of state. Life will go on." He moved closer and whispered into her ear. "Are you telling me you haven't looked around and thought the world would be better off without some of these people?"

"Well, I can think of a few I can do without," she spat back.

If the words stung, Dr. Reiss didn't show it. The progress monitor had reached one hundred percent, and the translation of the message on the Orb had begun. That beginning meant the end for Lara.

"I'm sorry to kill you, Lara," Dr. Reiss told her sincerely. "You would have been welcome in my world." He turned to the guard. "Take no chances. Shoot her between the eyes."

Upon hearing the order Sean gleefully yanked Lara's head up from the table, and the nearest guard raised his gun to shoot. *Blam!* A bullet went flying through two panes of glass and right into the back of the unsuspecting guard. Terry Sheridan had arrived on cue.

More shots followed. Quickly Sean and the doctor dropped to the floor, anxious to save their own skin. In the confusion Lara was able to leap up, grab her gun, and shoot the computer dead. All the information garnered from the Orb was gone. She dashed toward the Orb itself, grabbed it, and threw it into her backpack.

Lara raced for the door. Three glass panels stood in her way. Lara grabbed her gun and shot a hole through the glass in the first panel. The wall shattered, and she was able to leap through. She raised her gun again and shot a hole in the second pane of glass. She aimed her gun at the third panel and pulled the trigger.

Nothing.

She was out of bullets. And trapped. Lara had no choice. She dove at the wall. Just before she crashed through the glass a bullet came flying by, taking the pane with it. Lara was able to make it through without a scratch.

Lara shot Terry a grateful glance as the two made their way out of the lab and into the mall.

·"The elevators," Terry ordered as they raced through the halls.

Together they leaped into a nearby elevator that would take them to the surface. But Terry didn't push the button for the ground floor. Instead he pushed "110."

"Top floor?" Lara asked dubiously.

"Trust me," Terry assured her as he pulled the emergency button, ensuring that the elevator would stop nowhere else.

In the distance Lara could see Sean and about eight guards racing for the elevator, but they couldn't make it. The elevator doors closed without them.

That didn't mean they couldn't reach the roof. After all, there were other elevators. But Lara and Terry got there first. As the doors opened, they raced out and dashed into a small stairwell. Quickly they opened the roof access door.

Lara emerged onto the roof and looked around. She wasn't sure what she'd expected to find there—a helicopter or something similar that Terry had supposedly arranged. But there was no chopper waiting. Instead there were two small backpacks stuffed full of nylon.

"Parachutes?" Lara asked, worried. Parachutes would never work. They would simply drop them literally into Reiss's waiting arms.

Terry shook his head. "Something a tad faster," he assured her.

They sure looked like parachutes to Lara. But it was all they had. She could hear Sean and his men heading up the stairs to the roof. Looking out over the city, she asked Terry, "Where do we have to reach?"

"That ship." Terry pointed out to a freighter about a half-mile away in the middle of the harbor.

"Great," Lara replied sourly. The parachutes would never get them there. She studied the area around her. Already Sean's men had taken positions on some of the adjacent rooftops, trying to get a good angle on Terry and Lara. Things were just about as bad as they could get. "Backup plan?" she asked hopefully.

Terry shrugged. "Stand here and get killed." He smiled at Lara. "Why, losing your nerve?" It was a challenge.

Lara never could resist a challenge. "Please," she scoffed.

Gunshots rang out in Lara's direction. Terry was right.

They really had no choice. Lara jumped out into thin air, followed closely by Terry.

For a moment, the two were in freefall toward the ground, 110 stories below. And then, suddenly their packs opened, and giant wings emerged. Lara grinned. The packs had webwings. Those would let them fly far enough to reach the ship.

Lara didn't allow herself to relax until she was sure she was out of the reach of Sean and Dr. Reiss's other minions. But after a few minutes, she allowed herself to enjoy the flying experience. She and Terry sailed between buildings. The sun had barely set, and lights were going on in the buildings below.

They sailed along toward the harbor and over the water. Together they pulled their chutes low and slid right onto the freighter.

"Refreshing," Lara admitted as she shook off her pack.

Terry smiled and then took off in search of the ship's captain. The captain led them to their room. Lara stepped inside, while Terry stayed in the hallway, negotiating a price.

The first thing Lara looked for in the room was a shower. Sure enough she found one. It was small, but the water worked. That was a relief. After all she'd been through, a hot shower would feel really good. She removed her clothes, stepped into the tiny stall, and let the warm water trickle over her body.

By the time Lara was finished, Terry had entered the room. She found him sitting by her opened backpack, holding the Orb in his hands. The sight left her slightly uneasy. Despite all he had done for her, Lara still knew who Terry was. He was not someone who could be trusted.

"So this rock is the map," Terry mused.

"That's right."

"I've never seen anything like it," he continued. "Have you? It's quite beautiful actually. And . . . it's the only way to find that box?"

"Just think," Lara said as the two exchanged smiles, "you could tuck it under your arm and go right out the door."

"Window's better, actually," Terry corrected her. "Off the ship faster. Harder to track." He laughed slightly and put the Orb down. "Would I do a thing like that to you, Croft?" he asked.

Lara smiled. Being with Terry still held some excitement for her. And while she still would not let her guard down, it was clear that she was enjoying the tension.

Lara would not have been so amused if she knew what was going on back at the lab. At that very moment Jonathan Reiss had spotted something Lara had left behind. It was the answer to his demonic prayers. "Sean, have the field team assemble at the airfield," he ordered.

"Where are we going?"

Reiss lifted Lara's wireless Digi-cam from the floor. Obviously Lara had partners somewhere. They would come in very handy. "Lady Croft is going to tell us," he replied in an ominous voice.

But Lara had no idea that Jonathan Reiss had his hands on her equipment. At the moment her thoughts were somewhere else. She stood by the small window in the cabin and stared out at the night sky. Her mind was moving quickly, thinking . . . considering.

Terry woke and watched her for a moment. She looked especially beautiful, her long dark hair falling down the back of her white wrap. He walked toward her and tried to take her in his arms.

But Lara was quick. She grabbed his wrist and shackled him to the bed with a pair of handcuffs.

"Why didn't you shoot Reiss?" she demanded, all business. "He must have walked right past you in the lab."

"I didn't have a clear shot. And I had no idea where you were."

Terry was good, but he couldn't fool Lara. One look into his eyes, and she knew that their time together had come to an end. "I'll inform MI6 you've completed your service. You'll get your money and your life. Don't waste it."

Terry laughed in disbelief. "Now is no time to go splitting up, Croft."

"It is," Lara assured him. "Before you're in a position where you make the wrong decision."

"You want to leave, go ahead," Terry told her. "But don't pretend it's to save me. You're afraid. Afraid you might not be able to pull the trigger. Afraid of letting your guard down, letting anyone in."

But for once, Terry was wrong. "I'm not leaving because I *couldn't* kill you Terry," she assured him. "I'm leaving because I could."

Terry stared at her. "And what if you're wrong about me."

She looked over at him, her face expressionless. "Good-bye, Terry," she said as she collected her things and walked toward the door.

Terry smiled knowingly. "This isn't good-bye, Croft," he assured her.

CHAPTER THIRTEEN

It was morning as Lara floated into Taipei harbor on a small Zodiac boat she'd borrowed from the freighter. Although it was quite early the harbor was already bustling. The area was home to a whole neighborhood of houseboats. Inside each one families were waking up, having breakfast, and preparing for the day's work.

Lara scanned the harbor carefully until her eyes fell on a houseboat with a huge television aerial on its roof. That would do perfectly. She expertly steered her small Zodiac toward the houseboat and leaped aboard.

The family inside the houseboat, two elderly grandparents and their young grandchildren, seemed more than a little shocked when Lara burst inside and interrupted their breakfast. After all, the family wasn't used to uninvited guests who arrived in the early morning hours. And they'd certainly never seen someone like Lara, dressed in a tight black jumpsuit, and carrying all sorts of electronic gear and weaponry.

"Good morning," Lara greeted the family in their native Mandarin. "Might I borrow your television? It's important."

No one answered. They just stared at the visitor.

Taking that for a yes Lara began to disassemble the family's television set and proceeded to wire her cell phone into its antenna. In a matter of moments Lara had turned a basic television into a monitor for a wireless Internet station.

Quickly Lara placed the speakerphone part of her cell phone right next to the Orb. Then she pulled out her video camera and placed it on top of the TV. She was now ready for a videoconference with Bryce. She pulled out her photo chip, slid it into her phone, and prepared to send the images.

Within seconds Lara contacted Bryce. She could see him on the video, while the two communicated on-line.

"All right," Lara said. "I'm sending the last images of the Orb now. . . ."

"Got them," Bryce confirmed as the images flashed across his screen.

"Translate them," Lara ordered.

"Translating," Bryce confirmed. He waited a moment. "Done."

Lara's eyes lit up with anticipation. "Send the sounds."

"Sending . . . now."

The tones began. Lara could hear them over her phone. It was a very rhythmic set of sounds with no real discernable melody. Still, the beat was hypnotic, almost mystical. Lara stared at the Orb, waiting. And waiting. And waiting. "Nothing," she told Bryce finally.

Bryce shrugged. "Back to the drawing board."

But Lara wasn't so sure. The sounds were definitely the key. But something was wrong with the sounds she was receiving. And then it hit her. "The tones are being distorted."

"I don't think . . . ," Bryce began.

"There's a phase shift because of the phone line," Lara insisted. "The pitch is wrong!"

A strange look came over Bryce's face. He seemed almost disappointed at Lara's reasoning.

"Have you ever listened to your voice on a tape recorder?" she asked him. "It's the same thing. The sounds came through this speaker distorted. So either send me the file, or I'll bring back the bloody Orb. . . ."

"Sending it," Bryce said, sounding a bit reluctant.

"To be honest I'm surprised you missed that," Lara

remarked as she waited for the sound file to arrive in her inbox. When it did, she opened the file. Again a strange set of rhythmic sounds filled the air. It sounded barely discernible from the first set of sounds. Still Lara was sure that the Orb would be able to tell the difference. She stared at the Orb and waited.

Again nothing happened.

At least not at first. Then, suddenly, the Orb began to emit images. The projected pictures encircled Lara, wrapping themselves around her like a blanket. Lara began to feel as though she were no longer on the boat. She was far away, in the middle of Africa, holding the Orb in her hands. She struggled to move her body, but she was frozen in place. Only her hands seemed to be able to move. She turned the Orb slightly. Suddenly the images that had enveloped her began to move as well. Lara realized that if she were to rotate the Orb, the world around her would rotate accordingly.

Lara moved the Orb in a full rotation, and images of Africa began to overlap around her. She kept her eyes wide, searching for a landmark she might recognize—a hint as to where Alexander had hidden Pandora's box. But nothing seemed familiar. The images were growing stronger and stronger, as though the Orb were pulling her along, closer and closer to its home.

As unmistakable images of Mt. Kilimanjaro passed before her eyes, Lara noticed a mountain rising up from an African plain. The mountain stood so high it seemed to be swallowed by the clouds. As she seemed to move closer to the mountain she spotted a canyon at the edge of the jungle. Then she moved past a patch of barren rocky land, empty other than a few dead trees.

The images slowed down until they stopped completely. Now in front of her Lara could see a single cone at the summit of the mountain. Instinctively Lara knew that this was where she had to go.

But where was she exactly?

Lara turned the Orb, trying to get a better sense of the mountain's location. A blanket of darkness descended upon her. In the pitch black, she could hear a strange rumbling sound coming toward her. It was like lava bubbling deep inside a volcano. The sound was foreboding . . . almost alive.

Lara had the most horrifying sense that something awful was behind her. She tried to jump out of the way, but she was still frozen, the Orb in her hands. She gulped. Not being able to move was terrifying. The only part of her body able to move at all were her fingers. So Lara did the only thing she could—she moved the Orb around in her hands. But instead of freeing her from the mysterious, nebulous enemy, her actions only seemed to make things more frightening. Shadowlike monsters seemed to envelop her, sending a chill through her spine. Lara dropped the Orb in shock.

"Lara! Lara!" Bryce cried out.

Lara looked up at the video screen, nearly breathless. It had been a frightening experience, but well worth the fear. Lara now knew where she had to go. She knew where Pandora's box had been hidden for centuries.

"Africa. It's in Africa!" she exclaimed. "Somewhere past Kilimanjaro."

Bryce stared at her, emotionless. "That's great, Lara," he said in a flat tone.

"How long will it take Reiss to put his computer back together?" she asked.

Bryce seemed strangely uncomfortable. He struggled for an answer. "Twenty-four hours at the earliest," he said finally.

Lara nodded and set the countdown on her watch. "Then that's what we'll assume," she told him. "Get in touch with Kosa. Tell him to pick up my car and meet me north of his village!" Lara pushed a button and the screen went black. She had no more time for small talk with Bryce. She had to get to Africa.

* * *

As the computer screen went blank in Bryce's trailer, a thick Irish voice let out a small laugh.

"Bit faster than twenty-four hours, I'd say," Sean remarked, laughing. He pointed his gun a little closer to Bryce's back.

Bryce gulped and glanced over at Hillary. Lara hadn't known that her most trusted allies were being held hostage by Sean and Dr. Reiss. She had no idea that she had just given them the information they needed to destroy the world.

"Africa it is," Jonathan Reiss told Sean.

Dr. Reiss wasn't the only one hot on Lara's tail. Terry had already found her small Zodiac boat docked in the Taipei harbor. Now, as he stood there, surrounded by fishermen and other dockworkers, his eyes scanned the harbor, searching for a clue as to where Lara may have gone next. Like Lara he immediately noticed the houseboat with the large television antenna. There was no doubt in his mind that Lara had visited that boat.

Quickly Terry leaped onto the boat. The same Chinese family Lara had met during breakfast was now having lunch. Somehow the grandparents and their grandchildren

115

didn't seem all that surprised to have another unannounced visitor.

"I've lost my friend," Terry told them in their native Mandarin. "And I'm not sure where to go. . . ."

CHAPTER FOURTEEN

Kosa sped across the plains in Lara's Jeep. Once he'd gotten the call from Bryce he'd dropped everything and hurried to meet her. Of course, had he known who else had been listening in on the call, he might not have been so anxious to join her. As he drove past a spectacular view of Mt. Kilimanjaro, his cell phone rang. "Lara?" he asked.

"You cleaned my Jeep," she said.

"I know how you like your equipment," Kosa responded. He looked around. "But where are you? I can't see you."

"Don't worry," Lara replied. "I can see you. Just keep going straight and keep your speed steady."

Kosa did as she asked. As the car drove on, Lara looked down from the sky. The parachute on her back was open wide. She adjusted her course a bit to match the Jeep's route. As the car zoomed along, Lara guided herself over it and gently set herself down in the back. She smiled triumphantly as she cut away the chute. No one made an entrance quite like Lara.

"I don' t suppose you considered a more normal means of getting here," Kosa remarked. With the Jeep still on cruise control, and the open plain a straight line, Kosa moved to the passenger seat and Lara climbed behind the wheel.

"No time," Lara explained.

Kosa held on tightly as Lara sped through the African plains, treating the dirt roads as though they were a racecar speedway. "How long do we have before Reiss finds this place?" he asked.

"Hours . . . if we're lucky."

"Worse than I thought," Kosa said, sighing.

Lara studied the landscape. It had begun to look more and more familiar. Not too far away she recognized a wide mountain with its summit obscured by clouds. "Kosa, we've never been here, have we?" she asked.

"We didn't come to this area before," Kosa assured her. "Why?"

"Because I've seen that mountain before," she replied, remembering. "The box, it's there somewhere."

"The locals call that the Mountain of God," Kosa told

her. "There is a tribe that makes their home there. They might help us."

Lara looked at him strangely. *Might* help?

"When you see them, you will understand."

Lara parked the Jeep at the base of the Mountain of God. From there she and Kosa would be traveling on foot. They hiked as quickly up the mountain as they could. Before long, the air around them became smoky. The cloud Lara had seen had actually been a fog of thick smoke.

"To keep them hidden from outsiders," Kosa explained to her.

As they walked through thicker and thicker smoke, Lara began to notice bonfires burning. Through the blinding white smoke Lara was pretty certain she could make out some human figures.

As Lara and Kosa entered the village, a group of tribal members came near them. Lara studied their faces. Each person had unique and beautiful markings carved into their skin. Lara had heard of the African practice of skin carving before. The markings were vaguely familiar. They reminded Lara of something she'd seen somewhere before. . . .

The markings of the Orb!

It was obvious that the members of this village knew of the Orb, and of the power of Pandora's box.

Lara and Kosa weren't immediately welcomed into the

fold. In fact the leader of the village made it quite clear that they weren't welcome at all. He wanted them to leave.

Lara wasn't going back. And to prove it, she pulled out the Orb. The tribal members stared at it with awe.

The tribal leader spoke firmly to Lara in his native tongue. Kosa translated for her. "Leave this object and go. Never speak of it. To trespass on the Cradle of Life is to risk flooding the—"

"Men are coming for the box!" Lara interrupted him. "Unlike me, they won't look at it with fear or respect, they will open it. They want to use it. Now I am sorry if I have to disturb your gods to keep this from happening, but I will do whatever I must."

The tribal leader listened carefully to Kosa's translation of Lara's explanation. Then he looked into her eyes, trying to determine whether this outsider could be trusted. "Do you truly understand what you are doing? Are you truly prepared for what you will learn?" he asked her. "Some secrets must remain secrets. These are very heavy burdens, very lonely burdens."

"I am prepared, sir," Lara answered.

The tribal leader nodded slowly. "I will give you ten men," he told her, reluctantly. They will take you as far as they can. They will take you to the Cradle of Life. To the box."

"Thank you very much, sir," Lara replied, in the man's own language.

The tribal leader stared at her. He had to make her understand what she was up against. "No one who has ever gone looking for the box has come back. The land beyond the canyon belongs to the Shadow Guardians."

"Shadow Guardians?"

The tribal leader nodded gravely. "They do not sleep, they never rest. To them the sky and earth are meaningless. They move like the wind. Anything that walks their land will die."

"What are they?" Lara asked him.

"They came with life," he answered solemnly.

"From where?"

The tribal leader pointed up to the heavens.

A few hours later Lara and Kosa found themselves in the midst of the dark jungle as they followed the ten tribesman toward the top of the Mountain of God. Lara looked around her. The trees, the view, and the land all seemed so familiar. She'd seen them before. They were part of the images the Orb had shown her.

"We're getting close," she told Kosa.

One of the tribesmen nodded and whispered something to Kosa. "He says you're right," Kosa translated for her.

"The Cradle of Life lies near the summit. He wants to know how you knew."

Lara glanced down at the Orb. The tribesman was obviously impressed. "I will not turn back with the others," he told her in his native dialect. "I will go as far as you go. I will fight the Shadow Guardians."

Lara nodded as Kosa translated for her. "Thank you," she told the tribesman in his own language. "With brave men like you, we shall win."

The tribesman turned to Kosa. "She has a funny accent," he remarked.

"He says you have a funny accent," Kosa teased Lara.

Lara chuckled. But her laughter was short-lived. All around her animals were fleeing, running away from something Lara could not see.

But she could hear something arriving in the forest. The sound that was now accosting her ears was frightening—a low, mechanical sound, suddenly booming upon them.

The tribesmen stood tall, ready to fight whatever enemy was approaching. They looked to the left and to the right, but it was impossible to place the direction of the sound. And then, suddenly, it was directly overhead.

Lara looked up to see three helicopters. Reiss. There wasn't time to duck before gunshots rang out from overhead. *Bam!* The tribesman Lara had just been laughing with fell dead. As he fell, more shots rang out. Reiss's men began climbing down ropes from the helicopters, shooting at the tribesmen.

"Run! Run!" Lara warned.

Bam . . . bam . . . bam! The sound of rapid-fire machine gun artillery filled the jungle. Reiss's men were prepared to execute them all. Within minutes Lara and Kosa were left alone. Most of the tribesmen were dead; the others had fled to safety.

Lara looked for a safe path, but there was none. She and Kosa were surrounded. Reiss's guards raised their guns and pointed to a nearby clearing. Lara and Kosa had no choice but to do as they said.

As Lara and Kosa arrived at the clearing, Sean was there to greet them. He patted them down quickly, searching for weapons. Luckily he missed the butterfly knife Lara kept in the small of her back.

Satisfied that his side held the only weapons, he set about to get the Orb. Finding it in Lara's pack, he grabbed it and immediately handed it to Dr. Reiss.

Reiss studied the Orb and then looked at the markings on the faces of the dead tribesmen. "Primitives will do anything to please their gods," he remarked disdainfully. Then he turned his attention to Lara and Kosa. "Thank you, Lara, for leading me here. And for finding the Orb in the first place. I'm sure you are aware that if you hadn't found the Luna Temple, none of this would be happening."

"It crossed my mind," Lara replied ruefully.

Dr. Reiss smiled at her. "My getting the box is a foregone conclusion," he assured her. "However, you've seen its exact location. You can save me hours, even days. I'll make you a version of the proposal I offered you in Hong Kong: Help me, and I'll make it worth your time." He leaned closer to her. "Think about what I'm offering before you answer. The chance of a lifetime. The chance to find out how all of this began. Life, Lara, the origin of what we are. Don't tell me that's not tempting."

Lara smiled slightly. "That's what got Pandora into trouble," she reminded him.

Jonathan Reiss nodded. "I admire your resolve. They told me you wouldn't do it."

Lara looked at him curiously. *They?*

Lara flinched ever so slightly as Bryce and Hillary were dragged out from behind one of the helicopters. This was all her fault. She felt as though she'd been punched in the gut.

"And I told them you would do it, rather than lose two more friends," Reiss continued, his voice almost mad with pleasure. "These, your closest."

"Sorry, Lara," Bryce and Hillary apologized as one.

Lara thought back to her conversation with Bryce. He'd been trying to warn her then that something was wrong, but she'd missed his clues. "I should've realized you'd never mess up those tones by accident," she reasoned.

"Take us to the Cradle of Life, Lara," Dr. Reiss demanded.

Lara looked from her friends to Jonathan Reiss. If she killed Reiss, his men would surely shoot Hillary and Bryce. But the alternative was more drastic. The future of the world would be in danger if Dr. Reiss got his way. She couldn't allow that to happen. And neither could her friends. They gave her a very tiny nod to let her know they were behind her one hundred percent.

Slowly she reached for the knife that was taped to the small of her back. She moved her hands slightly, trying not to attract any attention to what she was doing.

"It's your destiny to see what's inside," Jonathan Reiss continued, trying to coerce her. "It would be foolish to stop when you're so close."

Lara clasped her fingers around the knife and prepared to strike. Surprisingly, it was Kosa's words that stopped her.

"He's right, Lara," Kosa coaxed. "It's foolish to stop. Especially when we are so close. Just through the canyon— remember? Such a short walk might save your friends."

Lara thought about Kosa's choice of words. Just

through the canyon . . . where the Shadow Guardians were. She glanced around at the many guards surrounding her. If the Shadow Guardians really did exist, they would greatly even the odds. "I'm up for a walk," she agreed finally, "if it spares my friends."

By twilight Lara and Kosa had led Reiss, Sean and his guards far into the jungle. Bryce and Hillary remained behind with the helicopters, under heavy guard.

One of the guards slammed Bryce and Hillary into a waiting chopper and ordered them to sit. The pilot turned to them. "Anywhere is fine," he told the men.

Bryce and Hillary glanced at each other. The pilot was wearing a helmet and night vision gear, so his face wasn't visible. But there was something familiar about his voice.

And then . . . suddenly . . . the pilot turned, smiled, and attacked the guard! In an instant Reiss's man was dead. Bryce and Hillary stared at the pilot in amazement, and confusion. Why had one of Reiss's pilots killed one of his own guards?

As the pilot ripped off his helmet and face gear, it all became clear. The pilot was Terry Sheridan—and he was in attack mode. Terry took care of every one of Reiss's guards who'd remained at the helicopter site. With them out of the picture that left Terry free to rummage through their equipment and take what he needed. He salvaged the best of their rifles and plenty of ammunition.

Bryce and Hillary exchanged glance as they watched Terry load up the rifle. They knew Terry and rightfully didn't trust him. He could either save them or kill them depending on who was paying him.

"Do you know where she's going?" Terry demanded of them.

The men didn't respond.

"Well, do you?" Terry demanded again.

"No, we don't," Bryce replied, finally.

Terry studied his face carefully, searching for any sign that he was lying.

"What are you going to . . ." Hillary began to ask.

Terry shut him up with a gun to his throat. "Is there any answer you'd believe?" he asked cagily. Then he softened his tone. "Don't suppose either of you can fly a helicopter?"

"I can," Bryce replied.

Both Hillary and Terry seemed surprised.

"I have one hundred fifty hours between simulators and models," Bryce assured them.

"And in the real thing?" Terry probed.

"Eleven," Bryce admitted, rather sheepishly.

Terry nodded slowly. "You're only going to fly it once

I'm gone, so . . ." He grabbed the keys to the shackles that bound Bryce and Hillary's legs and tossed them to them.

As Lara's most trusted friends went about freeing their arms and legs, Terry went back to piloting the helicopter. As the chopper lifted off the ground and soared above the jungle, Terry looked down, searching for any glimpse of Lara.

CHAPTER FIFTEEN

At that very moment Lara and Kosa were leading Reiss and his men through a dry riverbed within a canyon. They were no longer traveling through beautiful jungle foliage. This canyon was dark and twisting. Its walls loomed up high above them. Darkness had fallen, making the canyon even more foreboding.

The canyon was so narrow the group had to travel single file. It was hard climbing, but Reiss didn't mind. He was well aware that with every step, they climbed higher and higher toward the summit of the mountain . . . toward the box.

The canyon ended abruptly, and the group found themselves at the beginning of a petrified forest. It was completely desolate. A wasteland. The only light came from the moon and the flashlights. The lights cast odd shadows, which seemed to move through the petrified trees.

Eeayhh! Suddenly terrible screams began to echo through the canyon, startling everyone. The place was completely empty—at least it seemed to be. Where could the noises be coming from?

Only Kosa seemed to recognize the source. From the corner of his eye, he spotted a herd of baboons, aggressively defending their home. Lara nodded. It wasn't the Shadow Guardians.

At least not yet.

"Through here or not?" Jonathan Reiss demanded.

Lara took a deep breath. "Yes."

Sean gave Lara and Kosa each a hard shove. "Move, baby," he commanded.

As they walked deeper into the forest, the screams of the baboons became louder and louder until they were almost deafening. The shadows seemed to dance around behind the dead trees. Lara whispered to Kosa, "The trees. I recognize them. We're close."

Kosa didn't answer. Instead he looked around, sensing something the others did not notice.

"What is it?" Lara asked him.

"Listen."

Lara stood still for a moment and did as she was told.

There were strange sounds coming from the distance—low, rumbling sounds, like the distorted grumbling inside a volcano that was about to erupt.

Reiss and his men stopped and listened as the sounds increased in volume. Lara and Kosa exchanged a look. They had no idea what could be causing the noise.

"Keep moving," Reiss ordered.

As Lara and Kosa moved on, one of Reiss's guards was distracted by something moving behind him. He turned and tried to find the source of the shadows, but he could see nothing in the darkness. The guard moved closer toward the trees. Ugh! A thick black ooze dripped from the petrified branches. It was like nothing he'd ever seen before.

The sound was moving closer now. The guard whipped around, anxious to face this mysterious intruder. But as his eyes fell on him, he opened his mouth to scream. He was barely able to get a sound out before a mysterious, horrifying creature instantly took his life.

"What was that?" Sean demanded, as he heard the guard's short cry. Everyone in the group stopped short and turned to face the guard, but he was gone. Completely. There was no sign that he'd ever existed.

"You three!" Sean called out to a few of the other guards. "Check on him!"

The guards were not thrilled with that assignment.

Still, they turned and slowly backtracked to where their fellow worker had last been seen.

"Whatever they are, they're getting closer," Kosa whispered to Lara.

The group walked silently further and further into the petrified forest. Suddenly the sound of gunfire rang out into the night, followed by a chorus of screams. There was no doubt in anyone's mind that the three guards Sean had sent back were as dead as their comrade.

It would appear that the Shadow Guardians were more than a myth.

Sean ordered his remaining men into combat formation. But their movements only brought out more of the horrifying Shadow Guardians. One by one the shadows picked off the intruders.

The Shadow Guardians moved at incredible speed. Their ability to leap, jump, and even fly defied all laws of physics. They seemed invincible. Bullets penetrated them, but left no mark. To them humans were merely easy prey.

Jonathan Reiss was furious. He suspected Lara knew that this surprise ambush was a possibility. "What is this?" he demanded. "What are you doing?"

Lara stared straight at him. "Thinning the herd," she replied, throwing his words back in his face. Slowly she began to back away from the horrifying scene of carnage before her. Kosa, Sean, and Reiss followed her lead.

Lara and Kosa managed to take refuge against a tree. "The tribal leaders were right," Kosa told her, as they watched the Shadow Guardians pick off the guards one by one. "We don't belong here."

Lara tried to remember. "What did the tribal leader say about them?"

"They move like the wind," Kosa replied. "Earth and sky are meaningless. Whatever walks their land dies."

Lara listened as she watched the scene before her. She was especially intrigued by a frightened guard who seemed frozen with fear. He couldn't move a muscle. And although the Shadow Guardians were nearby, the guard remained untouched.

"Whatever walks their land dies," she mused.

Another guard raced in front of the passing guard. Immediately a Shadow Guardian leaped out and slaughtered him Lara's eyes lit up. That was it!

Whoa! Out of nowhere a Shadow Guardian popped up right in front of Lara and Kosa. Kosa turned to run.

"No!" Lara warned him. "Kosa, don't move!"

He looked over at Lara. She was standing completely still. Kosa followed her lead and stood his ground, refusing to even blink. The Shadow Guardian circled them, inching closer and closer, hoping to detect even the slightest movement. Finally the Shadow Guardian gave up the hunt and leaped away.

"They only react to movement," Lara whispered to Kosa.

"Then we better not move," Reiss hissed in her ear. He pressed his gun tight against Lara's windpipe. His aura of cool calmness was now gone. He wanted to be rid of Lara, which made him furious that he needed her to complete his mission.

Lara looked around. Reiss's minions were all gone now. There was no one left but she, Kosa, Reiss, and Sean.

And the Shadow Guardians.

"I know it's close," Jonathan Reiss snarled into Lara's ear. "I saw it in your eyes. Take me to Pandora's box."

"I don't know how," Lara muttered.

"Do it now," Reiss insisted.

"I can't . . ."

"DO IT NOW!" Dr. Reiss lifted his gun to her eyes and then slowly pivoted around until he faced Kosa. A shot rang out. The bullet hit the ground. Reiss smiled slightly as he watched Kosa blanch. "The next one will be higher up," he assured Lara. Then he placed the gun near Kosa's head. "Do not stop walking until Lady Croft takes us there," he ordered.

"He has nothing to do with this," Lara protested. "It was my idea."

Reiss fired another shot. This time the bullet landed dangerously close to Kosa's foot.

Lara stared at her friend. She was desperate to help him. And yet . . . "I am not worried, Lara," Kosa assured her. "Don't . . ."

Whack! Sean slammed Kosa across the face with the barrel of his gun. "Shut up and walk," he demanded.

Kosa looked off toward the forest.

"Now!" Reiss demanded. He fired another shot, right at Kosa's head. He missed, but only because Kosa had begun walking.

Lara cast her eyes all about, searching for something familiar. Then she spotted a cone of light-colored volcanic rock she'd seen before.

Kosa kept walking. With each step the Shadow Guardians seemed to be getting closer to him.

"I don't like his chances," Sean joked.

Lara didn't respond. Instead her eyes scanned the mountain, searching for the jet-black cone she'd seen before. Finally she spotted it not more than twenty feet away.

The cone looked exactly as it had when she'd held the Orb on the houseboat. It was made of black ash, and a dark ooze gurgled from the top. It seemed totally out of place, surrounded as it was by lighter cones made of volcanic ash. Lara was mesmerized.

The ever-growing sound of the approaching Shadow Guardians shook her back to reality. She could see Kosa walking ahead. The Guardians were coming for him now. But he didn't seem afraid. Instead he walked on bravely, his face strangely serene.

Lara had no choice. She turned to Reiss and Sean. "Give me the Orb!" she demanded.

Reiss looked at her skeptically. He took the Orb from its pouch, but didn't hand it over. "Why do you want it?" he demanded.

The Shadow Guardians were coming up behind Kosa like a tidal wave. There was no time for arguments. "You want to get out of here alive?" Lara shouted at Reiss. "You want to find the Cradle of Life?"

All powerful arguments. But Jonathan Reiss wasn't about to hand the Orb over. "Tell me what to do with it," he insisted.

Lara stared defiantly into his eyes. "No." In a flash she grabbed the Orb from Reiss's hands and leaped away.

Sean was fast. He grabbed Lara with a speed of a snake capturing a mouse.

Reiss's attention was now firmly focused on Lara. That gave Kosa the chance to stop walking and stand still. The

Shadow Guardians switched their focus from Kosa to Lara and Sean!

As Sean grabbed for the Orb, Lara leaped up and spun around in a complete circle. Then she used the Orb the way an Olympic track star would hurl a discus. The solid Orb smashed Sean in the jaw, and sent him reeling to the ground.

Sean rolled down the side of the mountain. The Shadow Guardians watched him move and prepared to pounce. He reached for his gun and aimed it at Lara, but was killed by the Shadow Guardians before he could fire a shot.

Lara ran off toward the black cone.

Jonathan Reiss may have been momentarily shocked by what had happened to his closest associate, but his mourning period didn't last long. He turned his own rifle on Lara as she ran. He cocked the gun, and put his finger on the trigger.

Blam! Kosa blindsided him and knocked him to the ground. The shot flew off, far from Lara.

Lara kept running, leaping from one smaller cone to another. She moved higher and higher until she finally she dove out and managed to place the Orb on the black cone.

The moment the Orb touched the cone, the two merged into one. Within seconds they began to disintegrate, as though they were made of soft ash, rather than hard stone. The ground beneath Lara began to melt as well, pulling her down as the earth beneath her crumbled.

Jonathan Reiss had come too far to turn back now. He leaped down after Lara.

Kosa stood alone on the mountain. Lara and Reiss had fallen into the earth. They were gone.

Gone, but not dead. Despite being sucked below the Earth's surface by a force stronger than anything they'd ever encountered before. Lara and Reiss were alive. The force of the Orb's disintegration had pulled them down into the tomb of the Cradle of Life.

The two landed with a thud on the hard stone floor. The shock of the fall was strong enough to knock the gun from Reiss's hand. Lara grabbed for the gun, but Reiss was quicker. He snatched it from her grasp and knocked her to the floor.

"You took us through them on purpose," Reiss snarled as he yanked Lara to her feet and placed the gun by her temple. He was furious. His face looked like a wild animal who had been provoked—his eyes were ablaze and adrenaline pumped through his veins.

"Wouldn't you?" Lara replied, matter-of-factly.

Click. Reiss cocked his gun. The sound rang through Lara's ears. "Don't think you'll be able to outsmart me," Reiss warned as he shoved her ahead, straight into the inner quadrant of the tomb.

Lara struggled to see as they walked through the labyrinth of volcanic rock that made up the inner quadrant. It was dark and shadowy, lit only by the sliver of moonlight that was able to slip in through a small opening in the roof.

With each step the combination of moonlight and shadows became more disorienting. It seemed as though the chamber was constantly changing shape. The effect was dizzying. Lara struggled to hold on to her perspective, but suddenly what was up seemed to be down. Left seemed to be right. It was hard to stay on her feet.

"There it is!" Reiss shouted out suddenly, breaking Lara's concentration.

Lara followed Dr. Reiss's pointed finger. There, ahead of them, was the chamber which held Pandora's box. The room was empty, except for a star-shaped pool filled with a thick, tarlike liquid. Floating in the pool was a small simple box.

Pandora's box.

Lara was surprised. It was hard to believe that a poison

so powerful it could destroy the world was held in such a plain container.

"Perfect isn't it?" Jonathan Reiss mused, as though reading her mind. "All that power in such a small container. The gods didn't need fire and brimstone to kill."

CHAPTER SIXTEEN

Terry Sheridan looked down from his seat in the helicopter and spotted a few flashlights strewn along the ground beside a sinkhole that lead straight into the Earth. "That's it!" he cried out to Hillary and Bryce. Quickly he fastened a rope around his waist and began to lower himself into the sinkhole. He moved quickly, hoping he could get there before Reiss got his hands on Pandora's box.

Terry had to move fast. Reiss was well on his way to getting the box. But he had no intention of dirtying his own hands to do it. "I see no reason to break with tradition," Reiss sneered as he and Lara stood at the edge of the pool. "I think a woman should collect the box." He kicked Lara's legs out from under her and sent her sprawling toward the pool of black ooze. He reached out his arm and grabbed her by the wrist, breaking her fall just seconds before she fell into the gooey liquid. "Go on," he demanded. A few strands of Lara's hair fell into the liquid, and instantly dissolved. This was definitely not a pool she wanted to swim in.

But Lara had no choice. She leaned out across the pool and reached for the box. Jonathan Reiss held her tight. For the moment he was the only thing keeping her just inches from falling into the pool and certain death. "Go on, take the box, Lara!" he demanded.

Lara reached out. Her fingers grazed the side of Pandora's box.

Her mind raced. Ironically the only one she could depend on to keep her from falling into the pool was the man who would certainly kill her once she'd retrieved the box for him. She seemed to be out of options.

Or was she?

In a flash Lara reached behind her with her free arm. She grabbed the butterfly knife she'd had taped to the small of her back and jabbed it into Reiss's arm—the arm that held her above the pool!

Reiss screamed out in pain and let go of his grasp on Lara. She began to fall into the pool. Reiss fired off his gun. Lara twisted in midair. Her legs knocked Reiss to the ground, while her arms grabbed onto the edge of the pool. She landed facedown, less than two centimeters from the black ooze.

Quickly Lara flipped herself to her feet and began running back through the labyrinth that had led her to the pool. Once again she felt confused, as the light and shadows played tricks with her eyes.

But there was nothing wrong with her ears. *Bam! Bam!* She immediately recognized the sound of bullets flying as Reiss let two shots fly from his gun. Lara leaped out of the way of the first bullet. But she wasn't so lucky the second time. The bullet hit its mark, grazing her thigh. A trail of blood fell behind her as she forced herself to keep running.

The confusion and the illusion kept Lara and Reiss from noticing that Terry had found his way out of the maze and into the chamber that held Pandora's box. He waited patiently in the shadows to see how it would all play out.

Terry stayed behind as Reiss followed Lara into the inner quadrant. Lara could sense that he was getting near her, but it was hard to tell just how close he was—and whether he was in front of her, behind her, or beside her. Everything was an illusion.

Reiss let out another shot; Lara leaped up and out of the way. She ran to the left. At least she thought it was the left. She might actually have been moving down, instead. It was impossible to tell as the streaks of moonlight and shadows melded the confusing labyrinth into one huge optical illusion.

Reiss caught sight of Lara. He pounced, certain that she was just below him. But the light had played tricks on him as well. Lara was actually above him. He flipped and fell to the ground, dropping his gun in the process.

Now Lara flew at Reiss, jumping down, then flipping up, and spinning around. She wasn't exactly sure which way she was flying, but somehow, she managed to crack Reiss right across the jaw with a swift kick.

Happy that Lara and Reiss were keeping each other occupied, Terry approached the pool of acid. The box was still floating there. He couldn't just walk away and leave it. That would have been stupid. And extremely unprofitable. Terry carefully extended his rifle and snared the box. He pulled it to shore and pocketed his treasure, no one the wiser.

The shadows in the inner chamber where Lara and Reiss were battling each other created a clear path for Terry to return to the surface. He could climb right past them and never be seen. Which was exactly what he planned to do until he heard something that made him turn back around.

Reiss had shaken off the kick from Lara and was back

on his feet, with vengeance in his eyes. He cocked his gun and came after Lara.

"So it ends. Survival of the fittest, Lara. And the wisest," Reiss said proudly.

Lara inched away from Reiss. She was purposely trying to maneuver him back into the chamber and onto a ledge over the pool of acid. They were so preoccupied with each other that neither Lara nor Reiss noticed that the box was gone.

Lara checked her position. And Reiss's. She needed him to move a few more steps. But Reiss wasn't going any farther. He had his gun raised and was ready to rid himself of Lara Croft once and for all.

"I don't think you're either of those," Terry said, stepping into the chamber to distract Reiss.

Lara took the chance to tackle Reiss. A single shot rang out from his gun as Lara drove him right off the ledge toward the pool of acid—but she was falling right along with him!

"He's right." Lara flipped Reiss so he was the one to fall into the pool. She landed on Reiss as if he were a raft. As Reiss sank into the pool of acid, Lara dove off him to safety.

"You're not either of those," Lara finished. Reiss clawed the sides of the pool to no avail. He sank down.

She rose to her feet and eyed Reiss's gun, which was lying just a few feet away in the dirt.

Lara heard Terry's footsteps approaching her. She could hear that he limped slightly. Reiss's stray shot had hit him in the leg. Terry smiled. He was glad that she was alive. He removed his backpack and took out a first-aid kit.

As Terry tended to her wounds, Lara noticed the box next to his supplies. She decided to say nothing until she could better gauge his intentions. After all, he had come back to save her.

Lara looked up at Terry. "Hillary? Bryce?" She hoped her friends were still alive.

"They're fine," Terry assured her.

"I'm not fooled you know." A smile crept across her face—her way of saying thank you. "I know the only reason you helped was to prove I was wrong about you."

Terry smiled back. Lara remained guarded, but began to believe there might be a happy ending.

"Let's get out of here," Terry suggested. He turned to lead Lara out and picked up the box with the rest of his gear.

Lara stood transfixed—Terry had no intentions of putting the box back. Her happy ending slipped away.

"Terry," Lara said warningly.

Terry looked at her strangely. "You're joking?" He paused for a moment. "We just leave it here when it is worth a fortune?"

"Millions of people could die."

Terry smiled, "No one will actually use it. You're being dramatic."

"Terry—"

"What?" he snapped. "You want to tell me again about these millions? It won't happen. And I am not going to leave this here on the *chance* it might. I served my country, then I served my time for going out on my own. I've helped keep *this* away from Reiss. I deserve my reward. I'm taking it."

Lara attempted to block his path, but Terry just laughed.

"You do have authorization to kill me. Better do it then. Because if you think standing in front of me is enough—" Terry cracked her across the face, completely catching her off guard. She stood motionless.

The smile was gone from Terry's face. He was now deadly serious. "You don't have it in you to stop me. All your beliefs, all your ideals—they're not real. I am. And you've loved me." A single tear formed in one of Lara's eyes.

"I don't care how strong you think you are. You're not going to choose them over me." Terry paused. "Now move."

But Lara would not yield—not the path blocking Terry's retreat, nor her beliefs.

"Fine," Terry smiled disarmingly.

The next instant everything was a blur as Terry reached for his weapon and Lara spun around.

Bang! A single shot rang out.

CHAPTER SEVENTEEN

Lara knelt by the pool of acid with Pandora's box in one hand. She was about to put the box back in the pool when the lid released ever so slightly, as if it were begging to be opened. She was alone; no one in the world would have to know. It was *the* mystery of the ages—the ultimate find for the ultimate tomb raider.

But Terry was wrong about her. Without her beliefs and ideals she was nothing. Lara placed the box, unopened, back in the pool. It drifted toward the center.

Suddenly a bright white light gleamed down upon her from a crack in the ceiling. It was an incredible beam— magical and full of hope. Quickly Lara headed for the light.

The source of the light filled her heart with love and

gratitude. The white light came from what seemed to be a hundred lanterns—all held by Kosa and the tribesmen. Lara looked at their marked faces and smiled gratefully. Then she looked to her friend Kosa.

"The Shadow Guardians. They're gone," Kosa assured her.

"The box is safe now," the tribal leader explained.

Lara thought back to something her late friend Gus Petraki had said to her that fateful morning when she'd first found the Orb in the Luna Temple. He'd said that perhaps the Temple was meant to be kept hidden. At the time Lara hadn't believed him. In true tomb raider fashion, she'd thought everything was there for the taking. But she'd changed her mind.

"Some things aren't meant to be found," Lara told the leader quietly.

She took a deep breath, thinking about how she'd killed Terry. Lara knew she'd had no choice, and yet the decision weighed heavily on her. Still, the Terry Lara had known had died a long time ago.

Lara turned to Kosa and nodded. It was time to move on.

A few hours later Lara found herself on a ledge just above the tribal village. She sat alone, watching the sun rise over the plain. Just below her she could hear Bryce and Hillary's voices. They sounded like they were having a good time.

Sadly Lara wondered if her own voice would ever sound that way again.

"Sometimes it's a lonely path," Kosa whispered quietly as he came up beside her.

Lara nodded slightly.

"But it is the right one," Kosa assured her. He looked down on the village. What he saw there made him laugh. "Your friends have made themselves at home."

Lara followed his glance. She could barely believe her eyes.

Bryce and Hillary had done more than made themselves at home. They fit in perfectly. Both men had had their hair braided by the tribeswomen. That wasn't totally out of character for Bryce, but for the ever-proper Hillary, it was positively mind blowing. Lara had to see this up close. She leaped to her feet and raced down toward the village, arriving just in time to see Hillary having his face painted by a large tribeswoman.

"That rather tickles," he said in his prim and proper voice, as she brushed the ink onto his face. Then he noticed Lara. It was the first time he'd seen her since she'd emerged from the tomb.

"Are you all right?" Hillary and Bryce asked her at the same time.

"Yes," Lara replied, choking back a laugh. "And better

now seeing the two of you. It's"—she searched for just the right word—"touching."

"You know us," Bryce said, suddenly embarrassed by his braids. "Always making friends, sharing a laugh . . ."

"Getting married," Lara added.

Hillary and Bryce both stared at her.

"This is a wedding ceremony," Kosa explained. He pointed to the two large women sitting beside them. "These are your brides."

The women smiled brightly at their grooms.

"B-B-B-But . . . ," Bryce stammered.

"I-I-I . . . h-h-how . . . ," Hillary added.

"Don't worry," Kosa assured them. "I'll explain this is a miscommunication." He turned to the leader, and began to speak to him in his native tongue.

As Kosa spoke, the tribal leader's eyes became small and angry. A vein popped out on his neck. He began to shout at Kosa.

Bryce and Hillary didn't have to speak the language to know the tribal leader was not pleased.

"Run!" Kosa ordered.

Bryce and Hillary leaped into the back of Lara's Jeep. She fired up the engine and took off, just as Kosa jumped into the seat beside her.

Lara floored the gas pedal. The Jeep sped off across

the African plains. As she drove, Lara could see the native animals roaming across their land, living their lives to the fullest. They had no way of knowing just how close their world—the whole world—had come to mass destruction.

But that threat was gone now. Hidden away in a tomb. Never to be found again.